BIBLES
BE
TRIPPIN'

JOCELYN & ALAYNE INGRAM

DEDICATION

This book is dedicated in loving memory to our beloved little cousin Whitney René Jackson. You would have loved this shit.

Yours in Faith,

Jocelyn & Alayne

CONTENTS

ACKNOWLEDGMENTS

We would like to thank our family and friends for their support. Well, the ones that gave it. Forgive them Father for they know not what they do.

Thanks to Philly for buying us the ISBN.

Thanks to R. Elliott for your valuable feedback and tips.

Most importantly, thanks to ourselves for this masterful work of brilliance.

1:26 And God said, Let us make man in our image, after our likeness: and let them have dominion over the fish of the sea, and over the fowl of the air, and over the cattle, and over all the earth, and over every creeping thing that creepeth upon the earth.

1:27 So God created man in his own image, in the image of God created he him; male and female created he them.

1:28 And God blessed them, and God said unto them, Be fruitful, and multiply, and replenish the earth, and subdue it: and have dominion over the fish of the sea, and over the fowl of the air, and over every living thing that moveth upon the earth.

- **Genesis, 1:26-28**

1 ADAM & EVE

In the beginning God created the heavens and the earth; which is weird because if He was already here, or there, what was He doing *before* 'the beginning?' Like, where was He? Was it dark? Did He eat? The world may never know. *On another note, the capital letters on "He" and "His" etc. stop now. That's too much to keep up with.*

Ah well, what *is* known, kinda, is that he created the heavens and the earth in just seven days. Kind of a big deal. On the seventh day, he looked around and saw how truly great he was. He had made the birds, the trees, the flowers and the bees, a host of animals, wildlife, water and we all know his famous coined phrase, "let there be light" and presto, there was light. Take that, Thomas Edison. But who would take care of all of this?

How was he going to give everything a name? There is only so much one can do after working all week. Creating the world is no easy feat and he was ready to sit the hell down and just chill, to the next episode. And so, on the seventh day, that's just what he did. Bedside Baptist ya heard?!!

God is an insomniac. He never sleeps nor slumbers - and he was bored. So, for his next venture, He decided to create a man in his own image to take care of the earth he had created. While he was still spent from a tough week of creating everything that has ever existed, he managed to find the strength and will power to create a man. He searched for the perfect clump of dirt and using that and pinch of the breath of life he created Adam.

Adam was a strong, handsome man with skin the color of holy oil; he was hardworking, smart and filled with unbridled enthusiasm. God saw that he was good. He decided that behind every strong man there should be a WOman, so using one of Adam's ribs he performed a suspect surgery, creating Eve. God told them that everything that he had created was theirs to grow and make flourish. There is just one thing you may never touch or eat from, he warned.

"Do not eat the fruit from the Tree of Knowledge; the day you do shall be the day you die."

Not literally, Adam lived to be 930 years old, as if that's even possible. His immune system must have been solid as a rock. It was more like one of those threats where people say, "OR ELSE!" Or when someone says, "If you do that, I'm going to kill you!" In this case, it was if you eat from that tree you will NOT live forever! 930 years seems like a pretty fucking long time to be alive.

In Adam and Eve's defense, why would God name it 'The Tree of Knowledge' and not expect Adam and Eve to be enticed? How about a little reverse psychology? 'The Tree of Death, Doom and Destruction' makes a little more sense. Was this all a grand scheme? If God is the master of our fate, all-powerful and all knowing, is this just an arguably well-written dramedy? Why even have a tree?

Anyway, Adam and Eve had a great deal of responsibility; they had to take care of the land, the trees, the birds and the bees all the while keeping a hectic and over-zealous religious schedule. They attended Monday night choir rehearsal, Tuesday night prayer, Wednesday night worship service, Thursday night Bible study and the occasional Friday night revival. They were so thankful to God for the life he had given them that they never complained. God was the fucking man in their eyes. Life was good for the most part. They rarely had any free time with all of the earth ruling duties and church obligations. They also didn't know that they were naked but they weren't aware that any other way of life existed. The lights were on, but nobody was home.

One day Eve decided to take some time for herself and skip out on noon prayer. It's not like anybody would miss her. Adam was busy doing only man on the earth things and the animals didn't speak the language. She took a long walk through many of the beautiful gardens until she came upon the Garden of

Eden. She walked through the Garden admiring its beauty and splendor until she came upon the Tree of Knowledge. She knew that God forbade her from eating the fruit from this tree but each piece looked like shimmering amazingness hanging from the branches. It looked sooooo yummy! Up to this point, she had never experienced a single temptation in all of her life. Still, she resisted.

As she turned to leave, a serpent twisted around the tree and said, "You can eat from this tree. I do it all the time and it is good! You won't die either, God just doesn't want you to know the truth about what's *really* going down."

Eve didn't believe him but there was no denying her curiosity.

"Go on, do it," said the serpent.

Peer pressure is a bitch because next thing you

know, Eve was going to town on any and every berry she could get her hands on. The serpent was right, it *was* good! She ran back to share the deliciousness with Adam. He took an apple from his wife and ate it.

All of a sudden their eyes were opened! For starters, they could see that they were both naked and suddenly feeling very exposed and embarrassed, especially Eve. A razor was in order. Adam looked around at the animals surrounding them and began to panic, terrified. He began to wonder how in the hell they were going to escape from these wild ass animals. He could just imagine the cowardly lion not being so cowardly all of sudden, attacking and getting a piece of his right ass cheek in his mouth. "Ouch," thought Adam.

He looked at Eve and said, "Listen, we have to get to a safe place. I hope you're in shape because I feel like we are in the jungle right now."

"So you expect me to run around flopping all over the place?" asked Eve in her bitchiest tone.

"Bitch, do whatever you want, I'm out," replied Adam as he took off running to safety.

When they got back to their hut or house or cave or whatever it was, they realized that they were still naked and something had to be done about that. They were very competitive people so they decided to have a contest to see who could make the best outfit out of five random things in the least amount of time. When God showed up, they were about to ask him to judge when he said,

"What hath thou done?"

Before they could roll their eyes because they hated when he talked like that, Adam and Eve realized that they had eaten the forbidden fruit. The blame game began; Eve blamed the serpent, Adam blamed Eve and then had the audacity to blame God because he created Eve and she had given him the fruit. It was a fucking mess.

God was angry; he told Adam that he might as well be Mexican because his future would be filled with manual labor jobs to survive. He told Eve that she was only going to be able to have children through painful childbirth and in addition, would have to bleed at random intervals for days once every month accompanied with intense cramping for her stupidity. To top it off, he also told her that if she or her daughters ever farted, no man would want them. Over-react a little more why don't you?

God told Adam and Eve that they were banned from entering the Garden of Eden ever again and placed two burning swords at the entryway. He must have gotten them from the sword factory that didn't exist and nobody worked at; he also was obviously an amazing fire starter.

It is rumored that because Adam and Eve were such epic failures and had given birth to the beginning of sin, God traveled to different parts of the earth creating other Adams and Eves in different versions. In Asia he created Adum Han and Eve Chin. In Africa he created Adamaki and Eveshina.

And the world was created.

The end.

4:1 And Adam knew Eve his wife; and she conceived, and bare Cain, and said, I have gotten a man from the LORD.

4:2 And she again bare his brother Abel. And Abel was a keeper of sheep, but Cain was a tiller of the ground.

4:3 And in process of time it came to pass, that Cain brought of the fruit of the ground an offering unto the LORD.

4:4 And Abel, he also brought of the firstlings of his flock and of the fat thereof. And the LORD had respect unto Abel and to his offering:

4:5 But unto Cain and to his offering he had not respect. And Cain was very wroth, and his countenance fell.

4:6 And the LORD said unto Cain, Why art thou wroth? and why is thy countenance fallen?

4:7 If thou doest well, shalt thou not be accepted? And if thou doest not well, sin lieth at the door. And unto thee shall be his desire, and thou shalt rule over him.

4:8 And Cain talked with Abel his brother: and it came to pass, when they were in the field, that Cain rose up against Abel his brother, and slew him.

- **Genesis, 4:1-8**

2 CANE & ABEL

Adam and Eve had moved on. They rarely spoke about what happened in the Garden of Eden, the tree of knowledge fiasco with the serpent, the burning of the swords or of being naked. If either of them ever brought it up, they would argue for days. Adam could always tell when an argument was coming; he knew her cycle almost down to the minute. Whenever Eve was on her 'bloody curse' she'd remind him of how he had called her a bitch. Once she started in, Adam could not help but bring up how stupid it was to take food advice from a random-ass, talking snake.

The past few weeks, however, had been pretty calm for Adam and Eve. They lived off of the land and were able to survive and maintain even without being in the grace of God. They were sinners now. Loners, rebels and had to get by with what they had at their disposal. Adam had made a bow and arrow out of some branches and twigs and was a pretty good shot; Eve was a fucking boss when she had a spear in her hands.

They had their fill of deer and fish but that alone didn't make for a happy home. Their sexual longings were not satisfied. They had been arguing so much that they hadn't really taken time to reconnect intimately following the whole banishment out of Eden incident. Adam decided to change that.

One day after hunting for the week's meals,

Adam came upon a beautiful patch of flowers he had never seen before. They were everywhere; their long, hollow, weed-like stems were skinny and green with dark brown roots. The flower itself was a vibrant yellow like Sunny D. Some were white and their petals more delicate. Any time a breeze would pass, little white balls of softness, yes softness, drifted from among them.

"These are extraordinary! Absolutely dandy. I'm going to call them dandelions," said Adam.

He began to pick the dandelions for Eve. This will be a great way to rekindle the flame we once had, he thought.

When Adam returned home, it appeared that Eve had the same thing in mind. There was a soft glow from a burning fire and as he approached, he could see

Eve sitting seductively next to the fire. She was wearing nothing but two berries over her nipples and a G-string with a solitary leaf to cover her own secret garden. He threw off his bow and arrow, laid his kill on the ground and rushed to present her with the dandelions.

"Eve, I love you and I'm sorry I've been such an obnoxious prick," he said.

Eve looked deep into her husband's eyes and said, "These are beautiful, thank you. And you're right, I am a bitch sometimes. I'm so sorry I'm such a cunt when I'm bleeding, I don't have any tampons and using leaves as pads gives me a rash. I shouldn't take it out on you. I love you too."

Adam pulled Eve into his arms and carried her into the bedroom. In the back of his mind he knew he was about to give her some good-lovin-body-rockin-knockin boots all night long. Eve was a trysexual, meaning she'd try anything once, twice if she liked it. This was his opportunity to try some of the stuff he had seen the squirrels doing. They put in work for hours and hours until finally they fell asleep in each others arms, exhausted.

Over the next few months, things were great. Adam and Eve were happy. Their tragedy was behind them and all things pointed towards a bright future. One day, Adam spent all afternoon hunting wabbits so Eve decided she'd clean herself up a bit. Her hair was ridiculously long and in need of a trim, (both sets), and she thought it would be nice to treat herself to a relaxing, warm soak.

As she undressed, she noticed that her stomach was sticking out quite a bit. She started to think, when is the last time I had to run out and gather leaves for my period? She couldn't remember and it suddenly dawned on her; she was pregnant. Eve began to panic; things had been going so well with Adam. She wasn't even sure if he wanted kids or if he could love her with all of the baby weight.

"Chill," she told herself. "Adam loves you and having this baby will be great. Shit, at least you know it's his, girl," she chuckled.

When Adam returned home later that evening, he saw the soft glow of the fire and thought, "SWEET, maybe we can do it 'bunny-style' tonight!" As he approached he immediately knew something was wrong. Eve sat near the fire trembling with fear and anxiety.

"What's wrong honey?" he asked.

"I'm pregnant," replied Eve.

"With what?"

"A fucking baby you moron - we are going to be parents."

"Wow! A baby, that shit's cray! I love you so much!"

Eve was relieved and Adam was ecstatic. He couldn't wait for Adam Junior to be here. He had already begun referring to him as 'AJ' and Eve couldn't be happier.

The time had finally arrived. It was time for AJ to make his debut into the world. Eve was going to do a home birth, natural, with no epidural, obviously since there weren't any hospitals. As soon as the baby came, they both saw the little beans and franks and knew they had a boy. Eve had been plotting behind Adam's back about the name because she had this great idea for a movie called, *Raising Cain*, and as soon as he popped out, she said, "His name is Cain!" Adam was so overcome with joy at seeing his first-born son that he didn't object.

Shortly after Cain was born they had another son that they named Abel. No cool back-story about how that name came about.

Growing up, Cain and Abel always had fairly different interests. Cain was a vegan at heart and enjoyed working with fruits, grains, vegetables and nature. Abel, being the meat eater he was, was more of a farmer. Vegans are weird and Cain was no exception. He could have been happy knowing that he was the first person to ever be "born" and not "created," but he wasn't. He was a sour-puss, bitch-ass, motherfucker.

Abel was an awesome dude in his own right. He had huge pecs because he did farmer shit all the time and he had a thick head of Bieber hair. He never even had to cut it; it just fell perfectly into place. Abel

felt like the only upper hand Cain really had was the

one thing he could never change - and it was just

coincidental, nothing particularly exceptional on his

brother's part. He thought about it often. He kept

himself sane with his motto, "First the WORST,

SECOND the BEST!"

Cain was a rebel to the whole first-born thing.

He was flamboyant; liked to wear skinny jeans and

pastels and Abel with his rugged good looks and Bieber

locks always had something to say about how prissy his

brother looked. They bickered about appearance

mostly. At the end of the day, Cain was just a bitch.

One day, God visited the family's homestead.

Adam and Eve were shocked to see him after all these

years. God was shocked to see they were still together,

divorce statistics being what they are.

"I have come to see Cain and Abel," said God.

"I will get them now," replied Eve.

I hope I don't fuck around and run into any serpents on the way she thought.

As Cain and Abel walked up to meet God, they shared the same, 'who the FUCK is this guy' look.

"Do not be fearful young men, I am the One who hath created this earth and the flesh of your mother and father, Adam and Eve. I want you both to bring me a sacrifice that shall be an offering unto me," said God.

Abel was pumped; he was thinking about carrying back a whole cow in his bare hands to show off his muscles. Cain was pissed, he hated competition and frankly didn't understand half of what God had said with all the shalls, hath, and flesh talk. All he kept thinking was, I was not out there planting my garden for THIS motherfucker to roll in talking about a sacrifice. Sacrifice these nuts.

Abel took off, eager to bring his sacrifice back to God. He would give him the first born of his best flock and some of the fatty pieces. Cain sauntered off to his garden to see what he could pull together. They had two hours to gather their offerings.

When the time had come, Abel stepped up and offered his gift. God was pleased.

"You have done well Abel. I bless you my son."

Cain had a tougher time deciding what to bring for his offering. He had just finished a lovely rose garden and had grown many beautiful flowers all around the house. He had also started a fruit, vegetable and grain garden with some of the biggest, most beautiful fruits and vegetables anyone had ever seen. He just didn't see how he could part with any of it for some dude he just met talking about blessings and sacrifices. Blessings? Be for real dude, he thought.

Cain stepped up and offered a few amber waves of grain and an arrangement of dandelions.

"What the hell- er, I mean what hath thou brought me? Things that mean nothing to you," asked God. "This is not a sacrificial offering. Be gone from my sight."

Cain was furious. Abel, the meat-headed muscle man, had stolen the show. He didn't even know why he cared so much about what this God guy thought but it really made his blood boil. Didn't God care about the animals that Abel had murdered? Helloooo - they were living things you prick. PETA would be hearing about this! His head was spinning. He ran back to his room, crying in anger.

Later that evening, Abel went in to check on Cain.

"You okay big brother?"

"I'm fucking fine, go away you over-achieving bastard."

"Whoa, what can I do? I'm sorry you are so upset."

Cain thought for a moment and knew this was his chance to get even once and for all. He smirked.

"Actually, there is something you can do. I want to make a better offering to God. I'd love it if you could help me pick out some of my best flowers and fruits," he lied.

Abel, being eager to rid his brother of his terrible attitude replied, "Of course brother, lead the way!"

Cain took Abel deep into one of his beanstalks. Abel wasn't the sharpest tool in the shed, he didn't have to be, he was hot and he had Bieber hair. He started getting suspicious as Cain began skipping through the stalks, whistling happily. All of a sudden he could no longer see him. He just heard that incessant whistle.

"Cain! Where are you?"

"I'm right HERE brother!"

And as soon as the word brother had escaped his lips, he plunged his diamond studded garden digging hoe into Abel's heart. Abel fell to the ground. Cain stood over him watching the life drain from his eyes. Abel was dead and Cain felt liberated. No more of this blessing bullshit. He had it coming, fucking farmer.

Cain returned home and saw his parents sitting around the fire with God.

"Where is your brother Abel?" asked God.

"The fuck if I know" said Cain. "Am I my brother's keeper? Wait, am I a gardener or a babysitting service? Stop projecting on me. First, you tell me to bring you something of MY choosing, and then you act all holier than thou. How do you turn away a gift? That's just fucking rude. It's not even your birthday; I was just giving it to you, stipulation free. I'm out of here."

God stood up, "Your brother's blood is crying out from the ground, you killed him!"

"So what if I did? It was his dumbass fault for following me out to the beanstalks. Who the hell just goes out into the creepy fucking beanstalks in the middle of the night, with a guy who is clearly unstable? I mean..."

"So this is just a big joke to you huh," asked God. "I'm going to put a curse on you and nobody will want anything to do with you."

God waved his magic wand and - oh wait, God blinked his eyes and twitched his nose - nope not right either. God just looked at Cain and told him, "I am going to put a mark on you so that everyone you meet will know that you are cursed."

And just like that, Cain was black. He could already feel himself changing. His lips were getting bigger. His nose a little rounder and his dick began to stretch out his pastel skinny jeans.

"Look what you've done," cried Cain. "If anyone sees me like this, I will be fucking killed."

"Oh no," said God. "I have something much better in store for you. You will be a slave. You will pick cotton until your fingers bleed. When and if that

time passes, you will have a tendency to be late and

hopefully you will be the token black anywhere you

go. Especially in movies. Sucks to suck"

 The end

19:1 The two angels arrived at Sodom in the evening, and Lot was sitting in the gateway of the city. When he saw them, he got up to meet them and bowed down with his face to the ground.

19:2 "My lords," he said, "please turn aside to your servant's house. You can wash your feet and spend the night and then go on your way early in the morning." "No," they answered, "we will spend the night in the square."

19:3 But he insisted so strongly that they did go with him and entered his house. He prepared a meal for them, baking bread without yeast, and they ate.

19:4 Before they had gone to bed, all the men from every part of the city of Sodom—both young and old—surrounded the house.

19:5 They called to Lot, "Where are the men who came to you tonight? Bring them out to us so that we can have sex with them."

19:6 Lot went outside to meet them and shut the door behind him

19:7 and said, "No, my friends. Don't do this wicked thing.

19: 8 Look, I have two daughters who have never slept with a man. Let me bring them out to you, and you can do what you like with them. But don't do anything to these men, for they have come under the protection of my roof."

19:9 "Get out of our way," they replied. "This fellow came here as a f. . . . . . . and . . . . the judge. . We'll treat . . . . . . worse than . . . . press . . . on Lo. . . . . the door.

19:10 But the men inside reached out and pulled Lot back into the house and shut the door.

19:11 Then they struck the men who were at the door of the house, young and old, with blindness so that they could not find the door.

19:12 The two men said to Lot, "Do you have anyone else here—sons-in-law, sons or daughters, or anyone else in the city who belongs to you? Get them out of here,

19:13 because we are going to destroy this place. The outcry to the LORD against its people is so great that he has sent us to destroy it."

-    **Genesis 19:1-10**

29

3 SODOM & GOMORRAH

Now this is a story all about how two cities got flipped, turned upside down and I'd like to take a minute, just sit right there, I'll tell you all about Sodom and Gomorrah being destroyed that year.

Contrary to popular belief, Sodom and Gomorrah were *thee* entertainment capitols of the world. And what many fail to realize is that the cities were actually located *in* California. It's unclear whether they were in the suburbs of West Hollywood or San

Francisco, but regardless, they had it going on. Their awesomeness is documented by these bangers: *We Love LA*, *Hollywood Swinging*, *California Love*, *California Gurls,* (they're undeniable), wish they all could be *California Girls*, *To Live and Die in LA*. Clearly, the place to be. Or so they thought.

On the outskirts, Sodom and Gomorrah had become solely synonymous with sex, drugs and rock and roll. It was rumored that the Bay Area had parades all day and the streets of Hollywood partied all night singing, "*All I wanna do,* is have some fun, until the sun comes up over Santa Monica Boulevard." Sweet *Californication.*

Yet and still, outsiders hated on the cities like Whitney Houston's sister hated on her in *The Bodyguard*. Or like Lord Voldemort, who's just a hater in general. OR how Scar's bitch-ass hated on Simba and

Mufasa, which was just, tragic. Ugh, *Noh8*. (PS - If you can't relate to at least one of those references, what is your life?)

Further out in wack-ass Bakersfield, CA lived 90-year-old, and some change, Abraham and his wife Sarah, who was also 90ish. The two were obnoxiously religious, very faithful to their country of 'merica, and hella old fashioned. They slept in separate beds like Ricky and Lucy. They had never and would never experiment with drugs or substance abuse because they wholeheartedly believed in the D.A.R.E. program, (it offers the skills and knowledge to avoid drugs and other arguably bad things like this book).

The only thing they were exposed to that was remotely similar to drinking alcohol or maybe popping ecstasy was the shot of 'the blood' they would drink and piece of 'the body' they would eat for communion every

Sunday. They did this to wash away the sins they never committed, obviously. They didn't believe in keeping a TV or radio in the house and wouldn't know how to operate a cell phone in case of an emergency.

Abraham and Sarah had become great friends with the mom from the movie *The Waterboy* and they all thought that damn near everything was the devil, especially Sodom and Gomorrah. They didn't want anything to do with that which they considered foolery and lived contently with their lame lives. The only connection Abraham and Sarah had to life outside of the church world was their nephew, Lot, who stayed with them while attending high school.

Lot was the odd one out of his classmates throughout his scholastic years. He basically stopped growing after 8th grade. He was very petite in stature and would probably get carded for the rest of his life.

He lacked facial, chest and even pubic hair. At 18, he stood at only 5'7" and weighed a measly 120 pounds. Most of the other guys towered over him. He kind of resembled a fairy with his short, brown, pixie hair cut styled spiky with blonde tips.

Lot was nice, smart and witty - but needed to break out of his shell. He wasn't shy, but he was a bit of an outsider - by default. He had a tough time truly being himself because of his Aunt and Uncle's strong beliefs. He felt like they would never understand and accept him for who he was, deep down, and he wanted so much more than this provincial life, (*Beauty & the Beast* - boom).

Things were especially tough when something excited him. For example, the other day when Abraham bought Sarah a new dress and they asked Lot for his opinion of it. Lot's eyes lit up and he started clapping his hands repeatedly screaming "FABU-LESSSS!" Abraham cringed every time he did this. The sight was practically unbearable.

Lot had never actually had any real guy friends. He had always felt an urge to get out there and bond; just be "one of the boys," but he just didn't relate with the guys at Bakersfield High. He wanted that to change and thought it might be a good idea to get into sports. He decided to try out for the school's basketball team.

He was a huge NBA fan and had hopped on the Miami Heat bandwagon after they took their talents to South Beach. He loved him some Chris Bosh.

Lot wished that he possessed the height and skill to make the varsity squad at his school. He must have made his wish at 11:12 because his tryout was a debacle. It went a little something like this: one forty minute game, (two 20 minute halves), 5 on 5 with the newcomers verses the starting five players from last year's team. Lot's first shot attempt was a wide-open three pointer from the corner. He got scared when the defense came charging towards him contesting the shot and threw up an air ball. The ball catapulted out of bounds and hit the coach's four year old daughter in the face Marcia Brady style. It took 10 minutes for her to finally stop crying.

He thought it best to get in a little closer for his second opportunity and drove the lane for a layup but his shot was pinned to the backboard by the team captain who grabbed the ball and shouted, "GET THAT WEAK SHIT OUT OF HERE!" He then went down the court for a fast break, 360 dunk, off one leg and pointed menacingly back at Lot.

Lot also struggled immensely on the defensive end that day. One time, the returning point guard, (whom Lot was guarding), brought the ball down the court and called for an ISO, which is short for isolation. It means that he recognizes that the defender's skills are sub par at best and wants everyone to see the offensive domination and impending defensive failure exposed at the same damn time.

Lot was cut following the possession having been given an Allen Iverson type crossover and thus, rolling his ankle. He was the weakest link, so... Goodbye.

Fortunately, there was still one more chance for Lot to join an athletic program at his school. He decided to go out for the cheerleading squad. If he couldn't play on the court, he still wanted to be near the action. It was the perfect fit. He was finally around a group of people who *got* him. The girls on the squad were so welcoming and it felt like they had a million things to talk about. Instant besties.

He was having a blast and before he knew it, he had graduated and was taking his pom-poms two hours away having received a full-ride cheerleading scholarship to UCLA. He was one of the top flyers in the nation and his high kicks were, as he would put it, "FABU-LESSSS!" Go Bruins!

When he finally settled down in Southern California he often frequented the Sodom and Gomorrah social scene. It was an intoxicating lifestyle, free of oppression and inhibition; there was no need to judge or feel judged, just love, and happiness. Something that can, make you do wrong. Make you do right.

Abraham and Sarah were proud that Lot would be furthering his education. They were disappointed that he wasn't recruited by USC and also, that he would be living so close to those God-awful, lust-filled cities.

One day, three angels came and visited the couple in Bakersfield. Abraham opened the door.

"Good morning, Charlie," the angels said simultaneously

"Whose Charlie?" Sarah asked, from the living room.

"Oops sorry, wrong story," the angels apologized and flew away.

One day, three FBI agents came and visited the couple in Bakersfield. Abraham opened the door. They were there to discuss the detestable acts taking place in Sodom and Gomorrah and the fate the cities were facing because of their wickedness. At this particular time in history, the line of separation between church and state didn't exist. Therefore, the public *could* be governed based upon organized religion. (Or something like that. Not really hip to politics but just go with it).

The agents said that the President was going to destroy Sodom and Gomorrah because the White House kept receiving terrorist threats and hate mail about the cities. The constant complaints were interrupting his private lessons that took place in the Oval Office with a few budding interns.

Normally, Abraham and Sarah would be all for this act of Patriotism, but because Lot was now living in that area, they couldn't possibly support the decision. Abraham asked the agents to see if the President would spare the cities if at least 50 people signed a petition saying they would get saved, (accept that God is Lord and that his Holy son, Jesus, died for their sins, blah, blah, blah). The President agreed, saying that he would not destroy Sodom and Gomorrah if there were 50 people willing to sign the petition and get saved.

Abraham realized this would be a hard task to accomplish so his numbers continued to fall lower and lower. He asked, what if there were 40 people, then 30. What if there were only 20 people who would sign the petition? Twenty dropped to 10. If Abraham could find 10 people in Sodom and Gomorrah to support his petition, the President agreed that he would not destroy the cities and subsequently, Lot could continue cheering.

Two of the agents flew to LAX to meet Lot who invited them to his studio apartment in West Hollywood to get this signage deal out of the way. Everything was going smoothly, they had picked up some In N' Out Burger on the way home and were chowing down on animal fries, just shooting the breeze, when the doorbell

rang. It was some of Lot's pals from Sodom. He had
met them at a bar off of North Robertson Boulevard.

One of his friends asked, "Where are those
hotties that you picked up from the airport?"

Lot stepped outside and closed the door so the
agents wouldn't hear their conversation.

"Bring them out with us, we need two more
guys to complete the orgy," they insisted.

Lot panicked. He realized that surely if he let his
friends try to holler at the agents, they would
immediately page the white house and blow this
motherfucker up.

"Look," said Lot, "there are two girls on my
cheer squad, one is the captain, the other is a freshman
this year, and they are both virgins but closet freaks. Let
me give you their numbers and you can sleep with
them. I'm not about to let you guys try to turn my guests

out. They're not like *that*."

Lot's friends were offended, pissed off, and hurt that he was trying to protect people that look down on them for their lifestyle. They demanded that Lot get out of the way. They called him a coward and a traitor as they inched closer and closer intent on breaking the door down.

The agents didn't know what was being said but they could tell that the men were arguing and the situation was escalating. One of the agents pulled Lot inside while the other sprayed pepper spray into the hallway in an attempt to temporarily blind his friends and stall for time. They asked Lot if he had anyone else here, a homie, a lover or a friend. Anyone else in the city that *belonged* to him.

They explained that they were really sent to save him and demolish Sodom and Gomorrah. They

43

had already set up boobie traps. Lot went out to try and save his only real friends, his cheer mates. He told them,

"Hurry and get out of this place because the President is about to take out the city."

They laughed and said, "Love you, you crazy bitch."

As dawn approached, the agents again urged Lot to hurry and take his people with him because the cities would be swept away. Lot grabbed two of his closest friends from the team because they were ride or die chicks.

The agents warned, "Flee for your lives, don't look back and don't stop until you get enough, keep on with the force don't stop."

They told the trio that they would be safe once they reached Valencia, California about an hour North.

They fled and the Government did in fact, drop bombs on Sodom and Gomorrah killing any and everything residing there. One of Lot's friends looked back, and she stepped on a land mine and exploded. Ouch.

The President and his agents were merciful to Abraham and Sarah by sparing their nephew. The destruction of Sodom and Gomorrah did not change who Lot was. The movement kept growing and as a result the Government planned to end the world in December 2012 or later, in similar fashion.

The end

6:5 And GOD saw that the wickedness of man was great in the earth, and that every imagination of the thoughts of his heart was only evil continually.

6:6 And it repented the LORD that he had made man on the earth, and it grieved him at his heart.

6:7 And the LORD said, I will destroy man whom I have created from the face of the earth; both man, and beast, and the creeping thing, and the fowls of the air; for it repenteth me that I have made them.

6:8 But Noah found grace in the eyes of the LORD.

6:9 These are the generations of Noah: Noah was a just man and perfect in his generations, and Noah walked with God.

6:10 And Noah begat three sons, Shem, Ham, and Japheth.

6:11 The earth also was corrupt before God, and the earth was filled with violence.

6:12 And God looked upon the earth, and, behold, it was corrupt; for all flesh had corrupted his way upon the earth.

6:13 And God said unto Noah, The end of all flesh is come before me; for the earth is filled with violence through them; and, behold, I will destroy them with the earth.

- **Genesis, 6:5-13**

4 NOAH'S ARK

Shit was getting out of control. God thought

about the whole forbidden fruit debauchery in the

Garden of Eden. The BS that had started it all. He was

so fed up with Adam and Eve at this point and it was

only amplified when Eve gave birth to black sheep,

hating-ass, murdering-ass, Cain. God's heart cried out

for Sodom and Gomorrah but the pure fuckery that had

escalated in California was absurd. That's not what he

had envisioned for the world when he had created the

heavens and the earth.

God knew that people had the choice to either follow the lame, extra-boring, straight and narrow path or enjoy life to the fullest. He just didn't realize that having a good time and enjoying life translated into crime, sex, drugs and that gays would be running rampant right before his very eyes.

God could see everything unfolding – every time anybody did anything, he saw it. He had the whole world, in his hands. Every time somebody was raped, he saw it. Every time the milkman made a stop at some housewife's doorstep, he saw it. Every time some flamboyant little twink bent over, he saw it. It was becoming extremely stressful and at times just fucking gross. Like, hey, loser jerking off to Jenna Jameson, God has to watch you too. There is only so much a guy can take before he reaches his breaking point.

Little did he know, his breaking point was fast approaching. God sat down to watch TV one day and decided to tune into TLC's regularly scheduled programming. His cable company was terrible so the guide didn't tell him what was on. When the show returned from commercial he was horrified at what he saw.

God exploded, "There is a reality series called Sister Wives?!"

He couldn't take it any longer. Not only were these damn, ungrateful humans destroying everything he had created but now dudes with long, shaggy hair were just taking as many wives as they pleased? Oh hell to the no!

God knew what he had to do. He had to set things right. He had to find someone that believed in

JOCELYN & ALAYNE INGRAM

him and was walking the straight and narrow. He knew just the guy: Noah.

Noah was a great man and disciple for the Lord. He had all of the qualities a person looks for when in search for a Godly man. He was kind, gentle, honest and just. Noah was married and had three sons, Shem, Ham and Japeth. He had raised his family uprightly and thought the violence and sin that had spread across the earth was despicable.

God knew that he would be the one to help him fix the situation. He was going to call this mission 'OperationWaterfall.'

Operation Waterfall had a lot of moving parts and while God knew that it would be a huge undertaking, he knew he was more than qualified and that Noah would be able to step up to the challenge. God called Noah and explained the situation to him.

"Noah, I have a favor to ask of you."

"Anything I can do for you Lord," Noah replied.

"I'm glad to hear you say that," said God. "As I'm sure you've noticed, the world is out of control and frankly, sex, drugs and crime have reached an all-time high. I'm going to destroy the world."

"I'm sorry, what?" asked Noah.

"You heard me, I'm going to wipe out the human race, all of the birds, the trees, flowers and bees. I'm going to start over and YOU are going to help me."

"Nope, still not following, come again," said Noah in honest befuddlement.

Did he really just say that he was going to 'wipe out the human race' or am I tripping? What the actual fuck? Thought Noah.

"I'm calling it Operation Waterfall. I am going to make it rain for 40 days and 40 nights. The flooding is going to be massive and destructive. Yes, I know that drowning is the worst way to die but honestly, people should have thought of that before creating shows like 'Sister Wives.' Have you seen that by the way?"

"Yes, it's a flipping train wreck," replied Noah. "What about my family?"

"I'm glad we are on the same page with that," said God. "Don't worry about your family. Because you are such a great and loyal servant, I will spare their lives along with yours. Also, we need them in order to repopulate the earth. Check your email in about an hour and you will find the rest of your instructions there."

Noah was shocked, worried and appalled but as

a loyal servant to God, what could he do? He had to step up and help God carryout his plans. He checked his email and saw the plans God had in store for Operation Waterfall.

Noah was to build a ship that would hold himself, his wife, their three sons and their wives along with two of every good animal and creature God had created. (Still trying to figure out how spiders made the cut). The ship needed to be massive, indestructible and most importantly, unsinkable.

Noah called his three sons and explained the situation to them. They began construction of the boat immediately. God's plans had been very specific on the length and width of boat. He also said it needed to have three levels and a window.

"We have to make sure that every safety and emergency precaution is taken," said Noah to his sons.

"I don't want any Jack and Rose Titanic type shit happening."

As they were putting the final touches on ship, Noah's sons asked him what he wanted to call it. It's customary for boat owners and captains to name their vessels and have the name painted on the sides. Noah wasn't a proud man but he WAS about to be the Patriarch of every family to come forever. He decided to call it, 'Noah's Ark.'

Once the ship was ready, Noah emailed God and told him that they were ready to begin collecting animals. He asked Him when they should be prepared to shut the doors?

God replied,

Dear Noah,

Operation Waterfall will commence in two days. Gather everything by then.

Yours in Faith,

God

Two days! I have two days to get things in order and ready to go, thought Noah. He and his sons set out to gather two of everything, a male and a female, of every creature and living thing that was *good.* (Again, how the hell did spiders make the cut?) Fuck.

By the grace of God, they were able to secure the animals necessary to recreate each population on earth following Operation Waterfall. While Noah's sons and their wives were in town saying goodbye to their friends, Noah was making last minute updates to the boat. He was checking to be sure that they had all of the supplies they would need for the next 40 days and 40 nights. He hoped that his sons and their wives stuck to the story they had rehearsed the night before.

They had been adamant about saying goodbye to their friends.

"If you must say goodbye to your sinner friends," Noah began, "you absolutely cannot tell them about Operation Waterfall."

"We wont," replied Shem's wife. "I'm going to say we are going on an exclusive family cruise."

"That's perfect and a great attitude and outlook to have in this difficult situation," replied Noah.

Noah was in his living room when his three sons came running into the room.

"Dad, we have a problem," said Ham.

"What is it son?"

"My wife accidently let it slip that God was going to destroy the earth and every human in it, *except us*," Ham replied reluctantly.

"She did WHAT?" Damn, broads stay running

their mouths.

Noah couldn't believe his ears. This was going to be like a reverse Titanic. Instead of people trying to get *off*, there was going to be a mob scene for people trying to get *on*. It wasn't as if he could hide the boat somewhere.

Noah looked at his sons and said, "Listen, tomorrow is going to be a fiasco. God is only sparing us so you must be ready to do anything necessary to keep these people off the Ark. Don't let it bother you though, it's like when people get trapped in snowstorms and they have to kill and eat one of their friends. It's ok because of the situation. Also, nobody will even know."

Noah and his family went to bed early that night knowing that their lives were about to change forever. His sons hadn't asked him the question that had been looming over his head since God first told him the plans for Operation Waterfall. I wonder when they will realize that we have to repopulate the entire earth, he thought. Troubling images of kids with Downs Syndrome and other horrific birth defects filled his mind as he drifted off to sleep.

Morning came quickly and Noah and his family were up and ready to go. They headed to the Ark and were greeted by an angry group of people.

"What the fuck is going on Noah?" one of the men in the crowd shouted.

Noah took a deep breath, grabbed his wife's hand and replied, "Do you want the truth?

"YES! We want the truth!" The crowd shouted.

"The truth is that you didn't make the cut and in about an hour you will all suffer a horrible death by drowning because your sinning ways are out of control."

That didn't come out exactly the way Noah had planned but he had gotten his point across. The crowd went nuts. People were flipping out. One woman was running around screaming about how she couldn't swim. An old man was on his knees trying to repent. Too little too late sucka.

Noah and his family started to enter the Ark. The crowd pushed forward, determined to be saved.

"God, help us," cried Noah.

All of a sudden a force field, real Star-Trek style, was between Noah's family and the crowd. It was like Noah had VIP access to the new, exclusive Club Ark and the bouncer wasn't letting anybody else in without family ID. That God I tell you, who knew he had a force field up his sleeve, thought Noah as he chuckled to himself.

Once Noah and his family were safely inside the Ark, they each went to their separate quarters to mentally prepare for what was about to happen. Shem's wife was a bit of a head case and seeing her friends in the crowd was a lot for her to handle. Get it together bitch, you made the cut. Move on. Noah told his family to sit tight and hold on to something when they heard the rain start.

The rain was soon upon them in full force. It roared and it wailed. They could feel the Ark being moved up and down, sideways and forwards. God was rocking the boat. This continued for 40 days and 40 nights. Noah was relieved that his family had been spared but was a little salty that he didn't really realize what he had gotten himself into. The stench from the animals was almost unbearable. They were two levels apart but animal shit is raunchy. Animal shit on a rocking boat, in cages, was just fucking toxic.

Spared from drowning only to be killed by the stench of feces, thought Noah. He couldn't wait for this to be over. His sons and their wives were always arguing. How the hell are we going to repopulate the earth when they don't even want to be around each other?

Noah opened the window they had built and sent a dove out to survey the situation. He had been working with this dove for weeks on various tricks and was confident that the dove would return if it wasn't safe. He was wrong. The dove didn't return and Noah knew that there was no way that it was time for them to exit the Ark. Poor dove, he thought.

"I wonder what happened," he said.

Poor dove is right. Noah was extra premature in his decision to send the dove out. God had sat down to change into his favorite Birkenstocks and had stopped the rain for a minute. The dove was feeling pretty good about the situation until the rain began again and wiped him out. Wrong place, wrong time buddy. Thanks Noah, thought the dove as it took its last breath.

Noah waited another week and sent another dove out. This time neither the dove nor the rain returned. He decided to wait another week for caution's sake. When he opened the window and there still wasn't any rain, he decided that it was time for him and his family to exit the Ark.

They opened the doors and stepped outside. The land was dry and bare. The enormity of the situation hit the family all at once. Noah's son Japeth asked the dreaded question,

"Umm dad, where are the people going to come from?"

"They will come from us son. It is our duty to be fruitful and multiply," Noah replied. "You and your brothers will recreate the population with your wives. My stamina ain't what it used to be."

Shem was shocked, "Dad, you do realize that somewhere down the line our close relatives will be sleeping together right?"

"Yes son, I do," replied Noah. "I've been doing some thinking and the best I can come up with is Kissing Cousins."

"That's gross dad," said Ham.

"Talk to God," said Noah. "Operation Waterfall clearly has a couple of loose ends."

Shem continued, "Now it's going to be our fault when somebody pops out a retarded kid. I don't know if I can handle that kind of pressure."

"It's too late to go back son. What's done is done. We have a responsibility."

God sent Noah an email when he saw that they had exited the Ark,

Dear Noah,

Good job! I know it must have been tough but I knew you could do it. I promise to never, ever, ever destroy the earth with a flood again! Pinky promise!

Now, your sons have some work to do! Tell them I said to give it to those women!

Yours in Faith,

God

Noah closed his email and breathed a sigh of relief. It was all over. His sons got to work and the earth repopulation began.

There was some other shit that went down later, some real family drama. Noah decided he was going to plant a vineyard and become a wine connoisseur. He got super drunk one night and passed out on his bed naked. His youngest son Ham saw him, took some iPhone video and posted it on YouTube. Shem and Japeth covered their dad up and gave the video the thumbs down on YouTube. When Noah woke up and found out what had gone down, he overreacted and cursed Ham. Really Noah, are you a sorcerer now? A wizard? No? Okay then, who cares?

The end

2:4 So Joseph also went up from the town of Nazareth in Galilee to Judea, to Bethlehem the town of David, because he belonged to the house and line of David.

2:5 He went there to register with Mary, who was pledged to be married to him and was expecting a child.

2:6 While they were there, the time came for the baby to be born,

2:7 and she gave birth to her firstborn, a son. She wrapped him in cloths and placed him in a manger, because there was no guest room available for them.

2:8 And there were shepherds living out in the fields nearby, keeping watch over their flocks at night.

2:9 An angel of the Lord appeared to them, and the glory of the Lord shone around them, and they were terrified.

2:10 But the angel said to them, "Do not be afraid. I bring you good news that will cause great joy for all the people.

2:11 Today in the town of David a Savior has been born to you; he is the Messiah, the Lord.

2:12 This will be a sign to you: You will find a baby wrapped in cloths and lying in a manger."

-Luke, 2:4-12

5 THE BIRTH OF CHRIST

"In the case of 2 month old baby Jesus-You are NOT the Father!" Joseph would never forget the day.

He had fallen head over heels in love with Mary the moment he saw her. She wasn't like any of the other broads he'd admittedly screwed over in the past. Mary was different. She had all of the basics covered; she was smart and stunningly gorgeous, and had an amazing gift to move through life effortlessly. She was like a deer mixed with a butterfly - graceful movements but also a delightful, fluttering spirit. If there was one downfall, she was rather *churchy* for his taste. The fact that she was still a virgin outweighed any negative qualities she might possess. His motto was, 'YODO: You Only Deflower Once!'

Joseph had just celebrated his 21st birthday and happy endings with drunk, hot girls were getting old. He knew he couldn't turn a hoe into a housewife. He wanted something new and fresh; something that would last.

Joseph devised the perfect plan after connecting with Mary on Facebook. Her dad had been looking for a handy man to do some construction work at their home. Mary told Joseph about the job, and then convinced her dad that he was the right guy to hire. Her father quickly took a liking to him and would always

say,

"Joey, you're going to make one hell of a carpenter

some day. Or maybe your son will, sometimes that shit

skips a generation."

In the meantime, and in between times, the two

took any and every opportunity to get to know one

another. Mary would walk around pretending to drop

things so she could bend over and show him what she

was working with. Joseph wore tight muscle-shirt tank

tops every day and would always oil up his chest and

arms so that his shit was glistening.

At that time, Mary was only about fourteen, but

her body was all Kim K. She was stacked and Joseph

was fully aware. His homeboys tried to warn him but

that butt she's got made him so horny. Sometimes he

felt like a pedophile but he truly loved Mary despite the

age gap. He figured that if he could get in good with Mary's dad, he wouldn't end up on Dateline's *To Catch a Predator* with Chris Hansen. He was right and the two started dating. Mary kept it pretty PG and blue balls and all he had to respect that. They were happy and their life together was beginning to take shape.

After about two years of going steady, Mary started to get a little thicker. Initially, Joseph liked her having the extra meat on her bones. As time progressed, however, she blew up like the Pillsbury Doughboy. It was not a good look. The two were in love and planned to spend the rest of their lives together in marital bliss but because they had never been intimate, Joseph feared Mary had slept with another guy and could be pregnant.

That's that shit he don't like. She denied it vehemently. Jewish girls don't sleep around-allegedly.

He desperately wanted to believe her but the only way he could be 100 percent sure was to take her on the *Maury Povich Show,* (a popular television series where paternity and lie-detector testing as well as shocking sex secrets are revealed).

Once on the show, Mary took a polygraph test to prove to Joseph that her cherry, in fact, had never been popped. The lie detector test determined that she was telling the truth. They exploded with happiness; doing chest bumps, walking around the stage waving their hands. Mary was jumping in Joseph's face pointing and screaming,

"I TOLD YOU! I TOLD YOU! NOW WHAT!"

When things calmed down, they hugged and took their seats. Prior to the show, Mary had been administered a pregnancy test and Joseph was given a paternity test. The DNA results were in. Mary was confident. Joseph - a nervous wreck. They sat, hands clasped as Maury stood to inevitably air out their dirty laundry in front of a crowded studio audience of their peers.

Joseph was not the father. Mary, was 16-and pregnant. Calls from MTV reps poured in. Mary could not understand how she could be with child and had never had sex. She talked to Dr. Phil, interviewed with Oprah, then, she went to see Dr. Oz. Nobody could explain this strange occurrence.

Meanwhile, Joseph was getting high as a kite because only in this state of nirvana could he come to terms with Mary becoming the mother of a child under such extraordinary circumstances. He sparked a second blunt and inhaled turning his squinted, red eyes toward the sky. He was so faded that he had an epiphany and heard a voice saying,

"Joseph, I am directed to instruct you concerning the son whom Mary shall bear, and who shall become a great light in the world. In him will be life, and his life shall become the light of mankind."

Joseph sprang out his chair and screamed, "Who the fuck is out here?"

Silence was all around him. Joseph looked at his blunt and said, "This shit is fantastic."

Shortly after, he shot Mary a text that read, "It's all good."

Mary's water broke at a barnyard rave Joseph had dragged her to in Bethlehem. It was pretty dark considering she went into labor at a party but luckily they had glow sticks. Although the lights made things seem slow motion and kind of trippy, the hint of flashing light actually helped more than it hurt.

On that cold December night, proud Mary gave birth to a baby boy.

"Name him Jodyyyyyy" one of the partygoers shouted.

She rolled her eyes and laid him in one of the leftover livestock mangers while they sat and thought up a name. Joseph wanted to call him Justin Christ. They went with Jesus instead realizing that one, Joseph must still be high off his ass to say some dumb shit like that, and two, yelling "JUSTIN CHRIST" in exclamation didn't have as much of a ring to it - and that's important.

After Jesus was born, three kings, Rick Ross, Jay-Z and Dr. Dre visited the baby bearing gifts of gold, frankincense and myrrh. They all bowed down before him. And thus, the Illuminati began. It turns out that Mary was a Delta Sigma Theta, so she had been throwing that dynasty sign up in the air for years. No wait, that can't be right. Mary was an AKA. Yes, *that* pink, *that* green. Joseph hated the color pink with a passion. He loved the movie, 'The Color Purple', but hated the color pink more than anything. His favorite color was red. So they decided to combine Mary's green and Joseph's red and that's where the Christmas colors come from. Obviously. Happy Birthday Jesus!

The end

17:45 David said to the Philistine, "You come against me with sword and spear and javelin, but I come against you in the name of the Lord Almighty, the God of the armies of Israel, whom you have defied.

17:46 This day the Lord will deliver you into my hands, and I'll strike you down and cut off your head. This very day I will give the carcasses of the Philistine army to the birds and the wild animals, and the whole world will know that there is a God in Israel.

17:47 All those gathered here will know that it is not by sword or spear that the Lord saves; for the battle is the Lord's, and he will give all of you into our hands."

17:48 As the Philistine moved closer to attack him, David ran quickly toward the battle line to meet him.

17:49 Reaching into his bag and taking out a stone, he slung it and struck the Philistine on the forehead. The stone sank into his forehead, and he fell face down on the ground.

17:50 So David triumphed over the Philistine with a sling and a stone; without a sword in his hand he struck down the Philistine and killed him.

17:51 David ran and stood over him. He took hold of the Philistine's sword and drew it from the sheath. After he killed him, he cut off his head with the sword.

- **1 Samuel, 17:45-51**

6 DAVID & GOLIATH

Life was becoming unbearable for David. His father, Jesse, was a Domestic Helper, which is just a fancier way of saying slave. (Similar to how people dress up being a Secretary by referring to themselves as an Executive Assistant or Office Manager). Whatever gets you through the day.

Anyway, David's dad was nothing more than a subservient. All he knew of his mother was that she had left his father to pursue a career in dance at Julliard.

77

And boy did she dance! She was making it rain dolla dolla bills at Lollipop's Gentlemen's Club. David was the youngest of 10 kids and was frankly sick of wearing hand me downs and living in the dusty shack behind the Millionaire's Mansion.

The Millionaire's Mansion was the shit. Equipped with flat screen TVs, a theater room, indoor basketball court, pool and each of the four refrigerators was always stocked with the finest, most exquisite cuisine and ingredients from around the world. It was a stark contrast to his life of sharing a room with his father, eating ramen noodles every night and having no choice but to wear Karl Kani and Fila to school.

The worst day of his young life was when he asked the most popular girl at his school to a dance and her response was, "Well I don't know David, are you planning to wear your Magic Johnson MVPs?"

David wondered when and if his time to shine would ever come. His seven brothers and two sisters had already left. Three of his brothers were involved in an underground fight club that he wasn't allowed to go near because he was only 14. The rest of his brothers were stoners and hippies who cared more about smoking weed, saving the whales, protecting endangered species and butterfly kisses. His two sisters had been sold into a sex ring straight out of the movie *Taken* when they were 15. He hadn't seen or heard from them since but he was pretty sure they were totally fine and had adjusted well.

One day when David arrived home from school his father was sitting in the kitchen with a worried look on his face.

"What's wrong Dad," David asked.

"I'm concerned about your brothers," Jessie responded. "There was a voicemail on my cell from Eliab and it sounded like he was in trouble. I need you to go down to the fight club and see what's going on."

David's eyes shot wide open. He was both excited and confused. He was excited that he would finally be able to see his brothers and possibly even *go inside* the fight club. He was confused about the fact that his father's cheap-ass, throwback Zack Morris cell phone accepted voicemail.

"What do you need me to do?"

"Just go down there and make sure all of your brothers are okay and don't need anything."

David ran to his room to put on his best outfit.

It was a tough choice between his stonewashed overalls and Magic Johnson MVPs or his black leather pants and Jesus sandals. Decisions, decisions. He stuck with his gut and chose the black leather pants because they made him look like a city slicker; he chose the Jesus sandals because they were built for comfort through wear, tear and tough terrain. He threw on his tuxedo t-shirt and grabbed his backpack. With one last look in the mirror he headed out the door.

When he arrived at the fight club, women in skimpy outfits were everywhere trying to pick up men, a homeless guy was walking around talking nonsense, asking for change, and cop cars were on every corner. The block was hot, hot, hot. It was a shady scene straight out of Oakland, California, (shout out to Tupac). David was instantly uncomfortable; he put his head down and headed to the back door. When he reached the door he knocked gingerly.

"What's the password," he heard through the speaker.

David was starting to freak the fuck out, how the hell was he supposed to know the password? He did what anybody with any common sense would do and decided to trust his instincts and most of all, to trust Ace Ventura, Pet Detective.

"New England Clam Chowder," he said.

He held his breath, did the Hail Mary cross the shoulders, forehead thing and crossed his fingers. Two seconds felt like forever but finally he heard the lock click and the door opened. David stepped inside.

"I'm looking for my brothers," David said when he got inside.

The room was occupied by four of the biggest guys he had ever seen.

"Well who the hell are your brothers? Do we look like mind readers?"

No, you look like King Kong's fucking brothers, thought David.

"Oh sorry," said David. "My brothers are Eliab, Abinadab and Shammah and they fight here

etimes."

The gorilla men looked at each and started laughing hysterically.

"Wait, so you're saying that those are Eli's, Abe's and Sammy's real names? Holy shit, was your mom fucking high when they were born?"

David was over this; he was pissed at his father for making him go check on his brothers, pissed at his stripper mother for naming his brothers those shitty names, (although he lucked out with David), and was furious that he hadn't chosen to wear his overalls.

"Look, do you know where my brothers are or not?" asked David.

"Yeah kid, they are in room number four; straight through that door, turn right at the first hallway and go all the way down."

Well fine-uh-fucking-ly thought David as he made his way to room number four. He knocked on the door twice and heard his brother Abinadab's voice,

"What's the password?"

Jesus Christ with the passwords!

"New England Clam Chowder," said David.

"The price is wrong, BITCH!" said Eliab.

"Guys open the door, it's me, David."

The door swung open and his brother Shammah stood there and stared at him in disbelief. David walked into the room and surveyed the scene. His brothers had been living the life; they had their own beds, a TV and a fridge. Snap! He looked over at Eliab and saw that he was in rough shape. The whole right side of his face was bandaged, he had a cast on his left arm and his left leg was mangled.

"What the hell happened? Dad said you called, are you guys alright?"

"Do we look alright," said Shammah. "Eliab is on his deathbed and we can't leave this room because some uncircumcised, giant mutant man wants to kill us. Eliab is our best fighter and he can't fight. If we don't beat him, we will lose everything including dad's house."

"You bet the house? How could you?" yelled David.

He was fed up with this whole situation and he was disgusted at the mentioning of the giant's "pig in a blanket" - gross. His anger fueled a new energy inside of him and he decided that he was going to fix this for his family and change his life forever.

"I'll fight him. Where is he?" David asked.

"Davy boy listen, it's nice of you to say but if we let you go in there, Goliath will kill you. I mean, his name is Go-lie-eth. Like if you fight him you will go lie down and not get up. He's a monster. This is not a joke," said Abinadab.

"I am going to fight him and end this," said David.

David left the room to find the man in charge. As he stepped into the hallway he heard a crowd roaring and walked towards the noise. He approached the arena doors and pushed them open. It was packed from wall to wall and in the center of the room was what appeared to be a boxing ring inside of a black net. David could barely see from where he was and couldn't even hear his own thoughts as the crowd began to chant. "KILL! KILL! KILL! KILL" they screamed.

David pushed through the crowd until he was in the front row and couldn't believe what he saw.

Surely this man-beast in the ring standing over what was now a clump of another man was Goliath. He *was* huge; hands the size of Michigan, (the mitten on a large U.S. map), arms and legs that seemed to go on forever and his head was big as hell. His forehead looked like a cream colored chalkboard. His shorts, if that's what you want to call them, looked like two California king bed sheets that had been custom fitted to stretch around his bulging thighs. Across his butt the word, "UNCIRCUMCISED" was stitched in red letters. Oh uncircumcised, thought David. It must be his thing.

The ringmaster grabbed the microphone and declared Goliath the winner. Goliath raised his arms in victory and was greeting by thunderous applause from the crowd. The ringmaster asked if there were any other challengers in the room.

"Anyone that beats Goliath will win $50,000 and be named King of the Israelites," he announced.

That's weird, what the hell is an Israelite? David didn't pay any attention to the last part of the prize, but instead thought of all the things he would do with that kind of money. He'd go see what all the fuss was about at Lollipop's, buy a pair of Nikes and probably buy a cool pick-up truck like the one J-Lo had bought for the back-up dancer.

"I challenge Goliath," screamed David.

Silence fell over the room as everyone stopped and craned to see who this brave challenger was. David stepped into the spotlight in his leather pants, tuxedo tee and Jesus sandals. It was as if everyone got a look at him at the same time because the crowd began to roar with laughter. David looked around and saw people laughing so hard they were choking. One guy had tears streaming from his eyes. A woman had fallen to her knees and her shoulders were shaking violently with laughter. He even saw an old man literally, rolling on the floor laughing, (#ROTFL).

The ringmaster invited David into the ring and told him to stand next to Goliath. It was an absurd image. A 14 year old kid in a ridiculous outfit next to a giant guy in sheet shorts with red stitching on his ass.

"What's your name young man?" asked the Ringmaster.

"David."

"Well David, the way we fight here is to the end. Are you ready for that?"

"Yes sir I am," replied David.

In his best Ryan Seacrest voice the ringmaster said, "Well in that case, dim the lights and here we go!"

David heard a bell ring and all of sudden Goliath was coming at him hard, with a vengeance. The look on his face said 'I'm going to kill you'. David backed up towards the net; as soon as his back pressed against it, he realized it was a stretchy, bungee material. He gave it a little test and put pressure on it and sure enough it pushed back against him. He had an idea. If I can just get to the other side with enough velocity, I could use the netting for leverage, David thought.

Goliath was approaching fast, with wild intensity in his eyes. Goliath reached to grab David around the legs and couldn't get a good grip on the leather, he was too slick. David scrambled to the other side of the ring and with all of his power leapt towards the net.

Goliath was furious; he had let David slip through his grasp. Goliath turned and began running after David; when they were about a car's length away from one another David propelled his body off the net and cocked back his fist. With all the pain from years of wearing the Magic Johnson MVPs, FILA and Karl Kani denim inside him he screamed, "ISRAELITES FOR LIFE" as he soared towards Goliath.

His fist struck Goliath in the center of his forehead with a smack. Goliath fell face forward onto the floor of the ring in a thundering thud. Dead. TKO. A drunk guy from the crowd came out of nowhere and yelled, "Goliath, you got knocked the FUCK OUT!"

David had defeated Goliath.

The autopsy report showed that Goliath had consumed a ridiculous amount of alcohol the day and night before as well as during the hours leading up to the fight. He never faced any real competition so he usually just got drunk as hell. Just what you would expect out of a Philistine. His high blood alcohol level mixed with the head trauma from David had killed him upon impact.

Not saying that's the only reason David won, everybody knows a 14-year-old boy can punch a giant man in the forehead and kill him. Still, he probably could've done it with just a stone and a slingshot.

The end

6:10 *Now when Daniel learned that the decree had been published, he went home to his upstairs room where the windows opened toward Jerusalem. Three times a day he got down on his knees and prayed, giving thanks to his God, just as he had done before.*

6:11 *Then these men went as a group and found Daniel praying and asking God for help.*

6:12 *So they went to the king and spoke to him about his royal decree: "Did you not publish a decree that during the next thirty days anyone who prays to any god or human being except to you, Your Majesty, would be thrown into the lions' den?" The king answered, "The decree stands—in accordance with the law of the Medes and Persians, which cannot be repealed."*

6:13 *Then they said to the king, "Daniel, who is one of the exiles from Judah, pays no attention to you, Your Majesty, or to the decree you put in writing. He still prays three times a day."*

6:14 *When the king heard this, he was greatly distressed; he was determined to rescue Daniel and made every effort until sundown to save him.*

6:15 *Then the men went as a group to King Darius and said to him, "Remember, Your Majesty, that according to the law of the Medes and Persians no decree or edict that the king issues can be changed."*

6:16 *So the king gave the order, and they brought Daniel and threw him into the lions' den. The king said to Daniel, "May your God, whom you serve continually, rescue you!"*

-Daniel, 6:10-16

7 DANIEL & THE LION'S DEN

Daniel and Darius were thick as thieves. They had been friends for years and couldn't have been an odder pair. Darius was a hard worker; he had put himself through college by working various odd jobs from the time he was 16 years old. He was a fat little fucker that liked to eat ALL the time but he was funny, genuine and cared deeply about the people closest to him.

Daniel, however, was born with a silver spoon in his mouth; come to think of it, Darius was born with a spoon in his mouth too. It had pudding on it. Daniel was rich as hell but still down to earth. He enjoyed doing things that normal, poor people did, like going to the movies, eating microwaveable dinners and using the RedBox. He was sort of a Jesus freak but he wasn't pushy or judgey; he just did his holy thing. The only time it became a problem was if they went to a sporting event and the team Daniel was cheering for did something good. His cheers always sounded like praise and worship. Sooooo embarrassing.

When they first became friends, Daniel liked to hang with Darius because he knew it made him look hard that he had a black friend with a semi-ghetto name. Darius also made him look extra hot when they walked into rooms. He soon realized that underneath all of that disgusting extra skin and behind the multi-colored stretch marks, there was a great guy with a huge heart. And ass, and hands and gut.

They had met when Daniel was a junior in college and Darius was the VP of National Connections International, Inc. At that time, the company was just beginning to expand into all 50 states and had plans to go global. Darius would always tell Daniel that when he became CEO, that he always had a job with him at NCI.

When Daniel graduated college, he contacted Darius and asked if a job was still available. As luck, (or obvious Godly favor), would have it, Darius had been named CEO and was in the process of reorganizing the structure of his company. He had created several different divisions and was planning to promote three people, that he would call "Super

Bosses" to manage the divisions. He had already filled two spots but the third one was Daniel's if he wanted it.

Of course he wanted it! Daniel thanked God for the wonderful opportunity and accepted the job. Over the course of the next few months, Daniel set himself apart from the other Super Bosses and was on track to be promoted over them. He wasn't sure what his new title would be but he hoped it would be something like "Super Duper Boss." He knew if he prayed really hard, God would make it happen. Or, as he had done so many other times, he would just buy Darius a bunch of his favorite foods and casually drop the new title on him. Ahh, fat people and their food.

The other two Super Bosses were haters. They hated how much Darius loved Daniel. They hated that Daniel was smarter, richer, funnier, more attractive and better dressed than they were. They hated that they were so insignificant that they weren't even named in the original story. They were basically like movie extras that were identified in the credits as "Guy 1 and Guy 2."

They had to figure out a way to get rid of Daniel. They plotted and schemed; had him investigated. Did a background check, looked into his credit and found old girlfriends. Daniel was squeaky clean. All they could find on him was a credit card, which was always paid on time, to Family Christian Book Stores.

"Jesus Christ he's lame," said Guy 1, er one of the Super Bosses.

"There has to be something out there on him. We will find it or we will create it," said the other Super Boss.

The company reorganization was almost complete and the Super Bosses knew they were running out of time. They needed to get rid of Daniel and fast! He was the clear front-runner for the Super Duper Boss position and they were not looking forward to that at all.

Their search for dirt on Daniel had come up short and they knew that in order to rid themselves of him they were going to have to concoct a bulletproof scheme. One that not even Scooby Doo, Shaggy, Fred, Daphne or Velma cold solve. Meddling kids.

"Listen, Darius is making his decision in two days. Let's go home and each think of a plan. I will call you tonight around 9:30pm and we can decide how we will proceed," said one of the Super Bosses.

"Sounds good to me, also, do you think you

could call me Aaron," asked the other Super Boss. "I realize that even though we didn't have names in the original story, it would be kind of nice now."

"Ummmm ok, Aaron it is. Call me Shaq-Diesel then."

Aaron and Shaq-Diesel went home with what felt like the weight of the world on their shoulders. They knew that time was running out and they needed to put together a plan that would get Daniel out of the way for good. **Precisely at 9:30pm Aaron's phone** rang, it was Shaq-Diesel.

"Ok, I think I got it man. We can take a bunch of naked pics of you and when Daniel leaves for work we can plant them in his house. It will be a whole gay fiasco. Darius may be fat but he ain't bout that gay shit."

The line was silent.

"Uh, hello," said Shaq-Diesel.

"Oh sorry, I was just fucking flabbergasted by that idea," replied Aaron. "That was absurd and quite possibly the worst idea I've ever heard. "

"Well shit. I thought I was really on to something."

"You were on to something. Something stupid and ridiculous. *I've* been thinking about ideas that actually might work," said Aaron. "So you know how Daniel is a Bible loving Jesus freak right?"

"Yeah, he was just talking the other day about how he got the praying hands tattooed on his back."

"Well, I'm thinking we can hit him where it hurts. We can convince Darius to make the workplace a no prayer zone for the next 30 days. And if people

must pray, then they can pray to Darius. Daniel prays

to God three times a day like clockwork. If Darius

makes that a rule, it will be grounds at least for

dismissal and maybe even worse, you know, like the

Lions!"

The Lions were the most notorious gang in the

area. They drove Hummers with tinted windows, wore

baggy, sagging jeans and bandanas. Scary looking

mofos. They could and i takin care of things that

law enforcement or law-abiding citizens couldn't. They

stole, cheated, raped, maimed and murdered but isn't

that what gangs do?

"Damn dude, you are way smarter than you

look. That just might work! I will stop at the bakery on

the way in and pick up Darius' favorite foods, pastries

and snacks and we will get this shit going," replied

Shaq-Diesel. "You get us on his calendar for tomorrow at 8:00am."

"And BOOM goes the dynamite!" said Aaron.

Both Aaron and Shaq-Diesel went to bed with a new peace and confidence about them. They knew that if they could convince Darius to put this rule into effect, poor little Daniel would soon face a terrible fate.

The next morning Aaron emailed Darius and told him that he and Shaq-Diesel needed to call an urgent meeting. Darius responded that he wasn't planning to be in the office until around 10:00am. Aaron wrote back and said they were bringing food; Darius hit him back and said "See You at 8!" Fucking fatties thought Aaron.

It was 8:15am and the meeting still hadn't started. Darius was stuffing his face and found it particularly hard to listen over the crunching in his head. He finally licked his fingers, sat back full and satisfied.

"Ok boys, what can I do for you?"

Shaq-Diesel spoke up, "Honestly sir, we have an idea that we think will help with staff morale, encourage bonding and really make them respect YOU more.

Darius sat up with piqued interest, "Ok, lets hear it," he said.

"We were just trying to think of ways to boost productivity across the board and make sure that EVERYONE is maximizing their time to the fullest," Aaron began. "We know we can't take away or cut down lunches or breaks but I mean we can regulate things like prayer. They don't even let kids say the

Pledge of Allegiance in schools anymore so why should we let people pray to God?"

"I'm listening," Darius replied.

"It's sort of offensive. If I'm walking down the hallway and I see somebody praying it kind of makes me feel a little funny," Aaron continued. "You know how if you walk into an apartment building and you smell a bunch of other people's cooking? It's like that, awkward you know. We need our employees totally focused if this company restructuring is going to work."

Shaq-Diesel chimed in, "Exactly! For the next 30 days, there should be absolutely NO PRAYING to anything besides you or NCI. That is the only way to ensure a successful merge."

"I don't know guys," Darius said. "It sounds a little fishy, ooh, fish sounds good. Anyway, do you really think it would help with productivity?"

"Darius, that is why we are Super Bosses, we work with the staff on a daily basis and know what kinds of distractions we should avoid," said Aaron.

"Okay then, let's give it a try," agreed Darius.

"Let's make it official sir. We drew up the document to go into effect in all employee manuals and handbooks. We just need your signature," said Shaq-Diesel.

Darius signed the paperwork and ended the meeting. He needed to figure out where he could order fish for lunch. Aaron and Shaq-Diesel could barely contain their excitement. They had done it! Now all they had to do was wait for Daniel to fall into their trap.

Lunchtime was approaching and Aaron and Shaq-Diesel casually walked past Daniel's office and looked inside. Daniel was deep in prayer; he must have been touched by the holy ghost because he was speaking in tongues, his eyes were a clear, crystal blue focused on something in the sky only he could see. His head, shoulders and arms were doing something that resembled a bank-head bounce. Oh yes, he was really feeling it!

"STOP! In the name of CEO Darius and NCI," shouted Aaron.

Daniel was so touched by the spirit that he wasn't even fazed by the noise.

"Umm, stop praying NOW," yelled Shaq-Diesel.

Still nothing. Daniel was only getting louder. He was actually jumping around clapping high then low and stomping his feet.

Shaq-Diesel screamed at the top of his lungs, "JESUS SUCKS!

Daniel stopped in his tracks.

"What did you just say?"

"We tried to stop you but you wouldn't listen. Drastic times call for drastic measures Danny," replied Aaron. "You need to come with us. You are in direct violation of the employee code of conduct."

"What are you talking 'bout?"

"Oh you'll see. We need to go see Darius now."

Shaq-Diesel and Aaron led Daniel down the hallway to Darius'office.

Darius looked up with surprise and joy. He always loved to see Daniel and was extremely pleased to see that Aaron and Shaq-Diesel were playing nice.

Everybody knew they smiled in your face all the while trying to take your place. Backstabbers.

"To what do I owe this awesome visit," asked Darius.

"Sir, we've come to report a violation of the code of conduct you signed into order this morning," said Shaq-Diesel. "We were just in the hallway and found Daniel praying extremely obnoxiously to his God."

"I got some of it on video on my iPhone if you want to see it. He was trippin' for a minute. You should've seen him," added Aaron.

Darius was pissed. He knew exactly what this meant. He had to make a decision. Either he had to stand by his word or prove to everyone that Daniel was, in fact, his favorite employee and that things were different for him. Shaq-Diesel could sense that Darius was wavering on what to do.

"If you don't make an example of him and show all of the employees that rules can't be broken by anyone, we will have an uproar among the staff," said Shaq-Diesel.

"Daniel, you have broken the rules of NCI. You have given me no choice. I am sending you to the Lions," said Darius, his voice full of remorse.

"The Lions? But Darius, what have I done so wrong?" Daniel asked.

"Just take him to the Lions. May your God protect you there."

By this time a crowd had gathered outside of Darius' office. Security stepped up and escorted Daniel out of the building into a black SUV. It was all very FBI transport-ish. Aaron and Shaq-Diesel climbed into the SUV. They couldn't wait to see Daniel being handed over to the Lions.

The drive seemed to go on forever. When they finally pulled up to the warehouse that was the Lion's home base, an uncomfortable, uneasy air filled the SUV. This could either be a smooth drop-off or the Lions could go nuts and start taking the wheels off the truck and shit.

Aaron and Shaq-Diesel got out of the truck and pressed the button outside the door. All of sudden they heard the lyrics of Tupac's "Bad Boy Killaz" playing throughout the building. The warehouse door opened and two burly men stepped outside.

"What the fuck do you want?" they asked.

"We are just dropping off a violator from NCI.

We will be back in the morning. If he's dead, he's dead. He's all yours," said Aaron.

The security guard brought Daniel to the entrance and shoved him at the two burly Lions. Aaron and Shaq-Diesel backed away from the door and jumped into the SUV. The security guard got back in the truck, clicked the locks and they sped away.

Daniel couldn't believe this. He was just minding his own business in his own office. Now he was at the hands of the Lions. He had heard stories of what they had done to other people for far less. Once, a man was picked up for jaywalking. When the Lions were done with him they had made sure he wouldn't be caught for jaywalking anymore, or any type of walking for that matter. They had cut off his legs, chopped them up into little pieces and made him eat them. The whole time they would taunt him, you like jaywalking huh? You like leg meat too? Daniel shuddered, this is going to suck.

The next morning came and it seemed like the whole town and entire staff of NCI had come to the warehouse. Darius stepped up to the bell and rang it. The warehouse door slid open and out sauntered Daniel. The people outside couldn't believe their eyes. There wasn't a scratch on him. As a matter of fact, it looked as though he'd had a fresh haircut and shave. He looked more rested than he had ever been. The people were wondering what exactly had gone down in the warehouse.

"How wonderful! Your God has delivered you from the hands of the Lions," exclaimed Darius. "From this moment on, we will all praise and glorify God!"

The crowd let out a deafening cheer.

"Bring me Aaron and Shaq-Diesel," said Darius.

Security ushered them both to the front of the crowd. They couldn't believe it. Their plan had backfired and they could both feel what was coming next.

"This is all your doing. I sentence you to the Lions and they may do with you what they see fit."

Aaron and Shaq-Diesel started flipping out. They had heard all of the stories and knew that this was not going to end well for them. The two burly Lions started dragging them into the building. The last words anyone heard from Aaron and Shaq-Diesel was a last minute plea from Aaron, "I'm allergic to leg meat!" And then the warehouse doors shut.

This shit was about to go down in history.

Daniel was the first person ever known to have escaped unscarred from the Lions. People wanted to know what happened. All Daniel would say was, "It was by the grace of God."

The real story goes like this.

Darius was fat as hell. That was a known fact. He wasn't stupid though. People often took him for granted because of his affection for food and round appearance. Daniel was brilliant and had hate-dar. It was like having gaydar where you can tell if someone is gay or not. His gift was seeing haters for what they were and stopping that shit before it got started. Both Darius and Daniel knew that Aaron and Shaq-Diesel were planning something. They just had to be patient.

Those two predictable motherfuckers basically fell right into their laps. After Darius met with them in his office he had called over to the Lions warehouse to see what they had going on for the next few days. They told him that things were pretty quiet and they'd be willing to play along. Darius promised them that they would be able to have some real, unhinged fun in exchange for their help.

Daniel was dropped off at the warehouse on schedule and all they had to do was continue along as planned until morning. It wasn't bad at all. He had pizza for dinner, caught up on some of his favorite TV shows and got a good night's sleep. He woke up early the next morning to give himself a haircut and fresh shave. He could hear the crowd beginning to gather outside the building and was pumped to get this show on the road.

Darius came to the warehouse door and Daniel sauntered out just as they had practiced. It was genius really – and they fooled everybody.

So at the end of the day, everybody was drinking the Kool-Aid. God was good and Daniel had been saved by his heavenly grace. It was *Biblical*.

Sike – flipping idiots.

The end

1:7 Then the sailors said to each other, "Come, let us cast lots to find out who is responsible for this calamity." They cast lots and the lot fell on Jonah.

1:8 So they asked him, "Tell us, who is responsible for making all this trouble for us? What do you do? Where do you come from? What is your country? From what people are you?"

1:9 He answered, "I am a Hebrew and I worship the Lord, the God of heaven, who made the sea and the land."

1:10 This terrified them and they asked, "What have you done?" (They knew he was running away from the Lord, because he had already told them so.)

1:11 The sea was getting rougher and rougher. So they asked him, "What should we do to you to make the sea calm down for us?"

1:12 "Pick me up and throw me into the sea," he replied, "and it will become calm. I know that it is my fault that this great storm has come upon you."

1:13 Instead, the men did their best to row back to land. But they could not, for the sea grew even wilder than before.

1:14 Then they cried to the Lord, "O Lord, please do not let us die for taking this man's life. Do not hold us accountable for killing an innocent man, for you, O Lord, have done as you pleased."

1:15 Then they took Jonah and threw him overboard, and the raging sea grew calm.

1:16 At this the men greatly feared the Lord, and they offered a sacrifice to the Lord and made vows to him.

1:17 But the Lord provided a great fish to swallow Jonah, and Jonah was inside the fish three days and three nights.

- **Jonah, 1:7-17**

8 JONAH & THE WHALE

Jonah was a fortuneteller from Galilee. His

stiffest competition in the psychic biz was Ms. Cleo.

Sometimes Zoltar spoke, but besides Jonah, Ms. Cleo

really was the who's who in the supernatural world. She

had come up with that catchy-ass slogan in her

mysterious Creole accent: "Call me now for your free

reeeadin'!" Shit, I can do accents too thought Jonah. She

prophesized in Nineveh which was a powerful kingdom

in Assyria - the dreaded enemy of Galileans. Her

clientele was very loyal and she had over 2 million followers on Twitter.

Jonah hated when he was compared to Ms. Cleo for a couple of different reasons; first, her accent was fake as shit. It was rumored that she was actually just some black bitch from Michigan that was trying out accents at a family gathering and it stuck. The second reason was because he was a *prophet*, not a fucking psychic. It's not like he was reading palms and pulling out ridiculous cards. His work was more of an art form; when he had a prophecy, it was like he left his body and was looking down on the world from the clouds. He had the glow, like in 'The Last Dragon.'

Jonah's boss, "G", was a well-known, powerful ruler. He was about his business and wanted to keep it in the family. His son Jesse along with his pal Homer would continue the legacy in the name of the father, the son, and Homer Goates. They brought Jonah in because he's what kept business booming. He was attractive yet unassuming. He had a confident air about him that made people want to hear what he had to say. Jonah was doing great in their home area, but they wanted to expand. They had most of Israel believing Jonah's prophesies but G wanted the Ninevites over in Ms. Cleo's hood too.

On Friday, at four-fifty-fucking-five pm, G told Jonah to go to Nineveh and tell all of Ms. Cleo's clients that they had best step correct because G don't like ugly. What this command translates to is, "hey, we *also* offer services, (to foresee what is in the future), like Ms. Cleo. Please refrain from doing what is convenient for you, and come join our movement. Or else."

It was time to clock out so Jonah was like "fuck that" and instead of following G's instruction, stuck to his original weekend getaway plans to Spain. His main issue with G asking him to speak to the Ninevites was that he simply didn't care much for the people of Assyria. Not only did they have beef from previous years but they were also ghetto as hell over there.

Jonah really didn't want the headache of chasing down his money; he was a prophet not a fucking collections agent. He wasn't trying to do all that extra work in the name of saving the world. Fuck the world, he thought. He would rather compete with them and see their business fail, as opposed to teaching them G's ways and thus, sparing them the error of their own ways. Basically, he wouldn't piss on fire to put them out; he wouldn't help them bury the body; he wouldn't take one for the team; he wouldn't shit where he eats. OK, not that last one - but you get the gist.

So, Jonah hopped on a plane in spite of his boss'

orders. He fell asleep shortly after departure and was awakened by the explosive boom of thunder. The rain hailed and the winds blew so hard the aircraft could barely keep straight. It was pitch black; then the lightning started with a flash and a bang of thunder. It was the perfect storm only without the sturdy boat captain getting drenched repeatedly as he continued to hold onto the wheel as if the waves crashing into him didn't hurt like hell. The flight attendant came on over the intercom,

"Ladies and gentleman, your captain has turned on the fasten seatbelt sign, please stay seated as we are experiencing a bit of turbul-ah, who am I kidding? This shit is about to drop like its hot and we're all going to die!"

Hysteria broke out in the cabin full of passengers. The Captain left the cockpit, yes, he left the cockpit during a storm, recognized Jonah as the famous

prophet, grabbed him and a few other men who were

seated in the emergency exit rows and said,

"Come, let us cast lots, that we may know for

whose cause this trouble has come upon us." (They

were all ridiculously superstitious and refused to use

words in the correct tense). They decided to draw

straws. The short stick fell on Jonah.

The men all looked suspiciously at Jonah

wondering what he could have done for them to be

experiencing such a terrible, awful, no good, very bad

storm. Jonah was extra defensive at first telling the men

to chill the fuck out and insisting it wasn't his fault.

"I can tell you're lying, because when you're

replying, stutter, stutter," one of the men exclaims.

Jonah hung his head and confessed that he was

supposed to be doing G's work but instead was flying to

a hostel to meet a young lady he had met online through

match.com

Jonah thought to himself, "how did I not see this coming," he shrugged, took a deep breath and with a knot in his throat said,

"Throw me overboard, into the sea. As soon as you do the storm will stop. Get rid of me and you'll get rid of the storm."

As Jonah is descending from the plane, all he could think was, "wow, those motherfuckers *really* threw me off the plane."

Splash. Jonah was one with the sea. Despite the vicious storm that was still underway, he managed to resurface. But as soon his head was above water, BAM something struck him in the temple and he fell into unconsciousness.

When he came to, he could see that he was in a

very dim room that was quite slimy, but hollowed. The first thing Jonah remembered seeing was what appeared to be a little, white volleyball with the name Wilson handwritten in red. Hmm, weird. Where am I? He thought.

He took a loop around his new surroundings and sees that the only visible exit is a small hole in the ceiling.

"Help!" He screamed. No response. "Heeeellllllp," he shouts again.

Still nothing. He runs to the nearest wall and pounds as hard as he can. It was squishy.

"Ew," he shouted, "what is this place?"

Two days pass and Jonah still didn't have any answers. He started to meditate. He pictured his crystal ball. It was a gift from G who had gotten it from the Wizard of Oz set. Remember when the Wicked Witch of the West Siyeeeed made Dorothy fall asleep in the

Poppy field? Yeah, it was vintage. Since Jonah didn't

have it with him, he had to use the magic 8 ball he

found. He shook it and asked,

"Where am I?"

"Yes, definitely," the ball replied.

Jonah rolled his eyes and chucked the ball at the

ceiling. It didn't come back.

"Whoa!"

He shot up, grabbed Wilson, and chucked him at

the hole too. He missed. He tried a granny shot and it

was good. Wait a second, Jonah thought. I *know* what

this is. Before Jonah received his calling to be a

prophet, he had studied to be a marine biologist.

After his third day of heavy meditation while

being submerged in the sea, he recalled what he had

learned about blowholes. That hole in the ceiling wasn't

just your average, everyday hole. It was the whales

nostrils which are located on top of the its head. The

reason he was able to survive for as long as he had is

because blowholes are covered by muscular flaps that

keep water from entering them when whales are

underwater.

Go fucking figure. Of course I was swallowed

by a whale, thought Jonah. I wonder if it's more Free

Willy or Pearl Crab-esque. Jonah knew just what to do

and he had modern technology to thank. He realized

that if this whale had been Willy or Pearl, they would

have definitely responded when he asked all of those

questions. No, this wasn't like any of the whales he

actually liked. It wasn't Moby Dick. It wasn't even

Shamu. *This* was a fail whale.

Jonah HATED when he would try to sign on to

twitter and that orange whale with the tweetie birds

popped up saying 'overcapacity please wait a moment and try again later.' Well, in this case, Jonah was over it and later was now.

He realized he had to make a decision. Either sit in the belly of the whale or get the hell out. He looked down at his hands with sorrow and did the unthinkable. He placed his hands on the whale's side and began to tickle the whale. It was squishy and disgusting, but it worked! Whales cannot breathe through their mouth, only through their blowholes. The whale began laughing hysterically and spat Jonah out onto the shore. Jonah jumped up soaking wet.

"Oh, I'm sorry sir, turbulence," said the Stewardess apologetically.

She had spilled water all over him. IT WAS ALL A DREAM. RIP Biggie Smalls.

The end

7:20 In which time Moses was born, and was exceeding fair, and nourished up in his father's house three months:

7:21 And when he was cast out, Pharaoh's daughter took him up, and nourished him for her own son.

7:22 And Moses was learned in all the wisdom of the Egyptians, and was mighty in words and in deeds.

7:23 And when he was full forty years old, it came into his heart to visit his brethren the children of Israel.

7:24 And seeing one of them suffer wrong, he defended him, and avenged him that was oppressed, and smote the Egyptian:

7:25 For he supposed his brethren would have understood how that God by his hand would deliver them: but they understood not.

7:26 And the next day he shewed himself unto them as they strove, and would have set them at one again, saying, Sirs, ye are brethren; why do ye wrong one to another?

- Acts, 7:20-26

9 MOSES

Detroit. Motor City. The dirty glove.

Motown. Greektown. Belle Isle. Home of the Lions,

Tigers and, *The Pharaoh*. Oh my.

He was thee American gangster; a drug Lord

who had perfected the art of smuggling everything

from Heroine, Cocaine and LSD to Shrooms, Opium

and Morphine. You name it, he had it. It was the mid

60's; a sexual revolution and he got motherfuckers

high. He ran the streets.

He was like the Midwest version of Alonzo from Training Day, (minus the whole being a crooked cop backstory but still just as intimidating, respected and powerful), with a slew of long lost pawns working for him. Everyone in the city felt enslaved. He was feared in the community but with the growing number of activists against him, and the potential for them to rebel against his reign, The Pharaoh needed to put the smack down.

He decided to put out an order to have all male children, born by any of his enemies or anyone who was even remotely against him, killed. Petty, but whatever.

That was around the time baby Moses was born. His mom wasn't down with OPP anymore so she hid Moses with hopes that he wouldn't be found and killed. She was able to keep him out of dodge for about three months but one night she had a relapse. Doped up on heroine, she put Moses in a crate and placed him in a dark ally. She convinced herself that she wasn't fit to be a mother and hoped someone would come along who could better care for him. Bitch, what the hell, who does that? Fiends.

Later that evening, in a deserted alleyway behind a bar, a young woman gave a young man fellatio. Or in other words: head/oral stimulation of the penis. As she bobbed up and down, her silhouette caused a shadow to reflect off of the streetlight onto the ally wall. That, paired with recurring moans and groans, caused baby Moses to cry.

"What the fuck?" The man exclaimed.

The woman released her jaw and turned her head to see where the noise was coming from.

Spooked, the man zipped up his pants, said he'd

call, and ran off.

"Wait, you didn't get my number," the woman shouted pitifully.

Disgusted, she took her handkerchief and wiped what she had left of him from her dress as she took a walk of shame over to the baby who had so rudely interrupted her romantic date. She picked up baby Moses and he stopped crying. She took him home with her that night.

The next day, she set out to find whom he belonged to. She went back to the ghetto near where she had gotten her freak on the night before.

Door to door she went, asking if anyone knew who the child was but all she kept hearing was,

"He ain't mines!"

After another hour of coming up empty, the woman was finally able to locate Moses' mom who

pleaded with her to raise Moses as one of her own.
Moses' mom recognized the woman as Sandra, a white
woman who had a history of scouting project rejects
and sending them to prestigious division one athletic
programs, like in the *Blind Side*. She also knew that
Sandra was the Pharaoh's daughter and had no business
being in that alley.

They made a deal. If Moses' mom would
continue nursing him until that stage was over, Sandra,
in turn, would raise him up right. Shit, it takes a village
doesn't it? His identity would remain unknown in her
father's home, and he wouldn't be killed. That was that.

Growing up, Moses was exposed to all sorts
of fuckery. The lifestyle that he had been raised in was
filled with promiscuity and substance abuse. It was a
social movement with new, improved drugs and sexual
liberation. At home, there was always a shipment

coming in to be processed or being sent out. There was rarely a time when someone wasn't snorting coke on the dining room table, shooting up or mixing chemicals in the kitchen. Business was constantly in rotation because everybody was just trying to get high to balance out the lows.

Moses didn't want anything to do with it but sometimes he'd have to chip in and make runs to the pharmacy to pick up undisclosed goods. He was trusted because he was the Pharaoh's "grandson" but besides drug runs, he wasn't affiliated. He gained an interest in medicine after one of his many trips to the Pharmaceutical plant and true to form, Sandra hired a tutor with a background in medicine to continue her pinky promise with Moses' real mom: to raise Moses upright and take care of his best interests. He would pursue a Medical Degree.

Moses knew that he wasn't a product of his environment. He was fully aware of who his real mom was, and that if Miss Sandra hadn't come along, it would have been a hard knock life, for them. Still, he hated how The Pharaoh and his crew treated the people from his projects. They were bullies and enablers who preyed on the weak.

One day, after a tutoring session, Moses took a walk through 8 Mile and saw one of The Pharaoh's men beating up a young kid from the same hood where he was born. Moses had no idea why this was happening but he knew it wasn't right. He got so pissed off. It was as if all of the injustice he'd witnessed in the city and in his old community over the years hit him like a ton of bricks. He approached the beat down, told the kid to run along, and killed the man.

Fortunately, he didn't have to go to court or

prison or anything like that. He got away with it because crime rates being what they were, police didn't have time to follow-up on each and every murder. Wait, what? I don't know, he wasn't black so they didn't have enough evidence to convict him or something like that.

The Pharaoh eventually found out about the murder and put a hit out on Moses. Moses realized that he was no longer safe in the D so he thanked Sandra for all she had done and fled to Lansing, Michigan. He figured he'd be safer living there because nothing ever really happened in Lansing. It's even sometimes referred to as "Lamesing" and just east of the city, is Michigan State University. Double negative. GO BLUE.

Moses had adjusted to the slow and much simpler pace of his new hometown. He had become very spiritual and developed a deep relationship with

God. He prayed constantly, mostly because there was nothing else to do there.

He decided to take what he had learned in his degree program and enter into a medical practice. He would spend the next 40 years fingeri.. er, as a Gynecologist dealing specifically with vaginal health and wellness.

One day while performing a routine pap smear, Moses' client told him that she had been sleeping around, unprotected, because condoms were for sailors, and that her hoo-ha was itchy and even burned sometimes. He was concerned but he always seemed to lose focus whenever girls came in unshaven. Her burning bush was throwing him all the way off.

Distracted, he began thinking about Detroit. He thought about his people at the hands of The Pharaoh. Moses suddenly became overcome with guilt for leaving, like a coward. He heard the voice of the Lord call out to him,

"Moses, do you remember when Superman decided to be human and make a life with Lois Lane?"

Obviously Moses remembered. It's a classic. God continued,

"Then tragedy befell Metropolis and he had to go back and save the day? Well, I'm calling on you; your people need you to deliver them from their plight. I will deliver them through you and you will lead them into a good and large land, with flowing milk and honey."

Moses tilted his head to the side in confusion at the last part.

"Look," said God, " I will be with you, tell them you are going to bring them to the promise land. March right up to The Pharaoh and say 'Let my people go.' He won't want to but tell him that your God will stretch his hand out with wonders against him and then he will let them go."

"What if they think I'm full of shit or if they don't believe that you're my homie?" asked Moses.

God reassured Moses that he had miracles and wonders that he would bless him with given the time and place to prove his almightiness.

Still reluctant Moses asks, "Well what if I stutter or don't know what to s.."

God interrupts, "Who has made man's mouth? Or who makes the mute, the deaf, the seeing, or the blind? Have not I, the Lord? Now therefore, go, and I will be with your mouth and teach you what you shall say."

Moses' mind starts racing, "But I don't know if..."

"JESUS CHRIST," says God.

"Yeah dad?" Jesus said as he came running through the heavenly gates.

"My bad J," said God. "I wasn't calling you, I just got annoyed."

"I know how that goes," Jesus replied.

"Look," God replied to Moses, "take your random brother, Aaron, (who is just now being introduced into the story), with you. He speaks well and you can convey my message through him. I will be with both of you and show you what to say and do. Since you lack self-esteem, you can be like how I am to you, for Aaron. Capeesh?"

Moses nods.

An expulsion of wind from the vulva snaps Moses back into reality. His patient had quaffed.

"That's all for today," he tells her.

Aaron and Moses drove to Detroit on a mission to overturn The Pharaoh. They were driving through a horrific snowstorm and black ice was covering the road, it was dangerous. Instead of it being the usual hour and a half trip it took them three hours to get there.

Cold and irritated they approached the bar where The Pharaoh was known to hangout. It was also one of his many fronts hidden throughout the city. They walked in the doors and even though they stuck out like sore thumbs, it didn't bother them one bit. They knew what they had to do and were prepared to do it.

The Pharaoh was there decked out in a full chinchilla suit looking like an over-the-top pimp. He was in the middle of telling his workers that he didn't

144

care if there was a blizzard, they better get out there and make that money when he noticed Aaron and Moses had entered the room. Aaron and Moses walked towards him and both said,

"Let my people go."

The Pharaoh didn't even blink. The corners of his mouth curved into an evil smile that said, "nigga please." At that moment, God provided his first miracle.

Out of nowhere, somebody started dropping a beat. Aaron clears space and starts poppin' and lockin'. It's as if the Holy Ghost had taken over his whole body and he begins steppin' Stomp the Yard style. Moments later he drops into a full split, crosses his arms and shouts, "YEAH."

Several of The Pharaoh's entourage retaliates

breaking into the epic Michael Jackson *Thriller* routine. It was a bold move and they nailed it. Moses decided that round three was his. He stepped into the circle and did a medley of backhand springs, round offs and cartwheels and the people in the crowded bar went wild.

Even though his team had proved to be incompetent in the dance battle, The Pharaoh still refused to let the people go. Because The Pharaoh didn't cooperate, God released 10 powerful judgments against the him and his people: Chlamydia, Gonorrhea, Syphilis, Lice, Crabs, Yeast Infections, Scabies, HPV, Herpes, and Massive Diarrhea.

The Pharaoh could deal with a lot of things but Lice and Crabs? No way, no how. He thought for a minute and said,

"Fuck it, they can go."

Moses and Aaron began to herd people out of Motown before The Pharaoh reconsidered his decision. They knew that they had to move fast. They were right because The Pharaoh did change his mind and ordered his crew to capture the people and bring them back.

He also ordered his crew to sign up for Hip-Hop Dance Classes because he was fucking furious at how they had embarrassed him at the bar.

The people of Detroit had a considerable head start on The Pharaoh's men but hit a roadblock at the Red Sea - also known as the Detroit River. It was the border between Canada and the United States dividing Detroit and Ontario - The Promise Land. Drake is from there.

They had nowhere to go. If they turned around,

they would be enslaved and treated 10 times worse than before. If they went forward, surely they'd drown. They needed a miracle, and there can be miracles, when you believe.

Moses stood in front of the crowd and said, "Relax y'all. I've got this."

As he stretched his hand over the Sea, the anointing of God was upon him. The people couldn't believe their eyes. The Detroit River parted like a fresh perm. The water was like a wall to the left and right of them and beneath their feet, dry ground. They ran to the other side. The Pharaoh's entourage were also in disbelief but ran after them anyway. As soon as Moses and his people had crossed, God told Moses,

"Stretch out your hand over the sea, that the waters may return upon the enemy."

Moses did as he was instructed and The Pharaoh's men drowned. To celebrate the victory, and the irony of their enemy's death by drowning, Moses took everyone that had crossed with him to the Celine Dion concert where she performed three encores of My Heart Will Go On from the blockbuster film, *Titanic*.

The end

22:14 When the hour came, Jesus and his apostles reclined at the table.

22:15 And he said to them, "I have eagerly desired to eat this Passover with you before I suffer.

22:16 For I tell you, I will not eat it again until it finds fulfillment in the kingdom of God."

22:17 After taking the cup, he gave thanks and said, "Take this and divide it among you.

22:18 For I tell you I will not drink again of the fruit of the vine until the kingdom of God comes."

22:19 And he took bread, gave thanks and broke it, and gave it to them, saying, "This is my body given for you; do this in remembrance of me."

22:20 In the same way, after the supper he took the cup, saying, "This cup is the new covenant in my blood, which is poured out for you.

22:21 But the hand of him who is going to betray me is with mine on the table. 22:22 The Son of Man will go as it has been decreed, but woe to that man who betrays him."

22:23 They began to question among themselves which of them it might be who would do this.

-Luke 22:1-23

10 THE CRUCIFIXION & RESURRECTION

All this has happened before and it will all happen again. This time it happened in Jerusalem. It happened on a quiet street in Neverland. Twelve lost boys, all Disciples of Christ, headed second star to the right and on till morning to a dive bar just outside of the old city. Jesus chose this particular pub because there were people there who believed in him.

- Back track -

One day, the lost boys were out being boys and

getting lost when collectively they decided they needed some direction. They sought out Jonah for some wise words but weren't fulfilled with his prophecies. Jonah told the boys that there was someone even more profound than he, and that he believed they needed to meet him. Jonah then handed over a map and a pair of ruby red sneakers and said, "Tell him I sent you."

The lost boys found God on the corner of first and Amistad. They asked where he had been and God replied, "Ask anything." The boys huddled up to discuss their options.

Peter whispered, "Hey, I've got my iPod on me, why don't we play 50 Cent's "21 Questions" for God?

"Good answer, good answer," Luke applauded.

"What? No," said Paul. "This isn't Family Feud. We're not answering to Steve Harvey here; this is the Lord God strong and mighty, the Lord that's mighty in battle. We've got to come up with something legit."

"Not necessarily," replied Luke. "What if God is one of us? Just a slob like one of us. Just a stranger, on a bus. Trying to make his way home."

"Dude, shut the fuck up, Jesus!" Paul exclaimed.

They all stood and thought for a moment.

"Hey, that's it," said Mark. "Let's ask God about Jesus. I heard his mom is a virgin. I'm still confused about that shit."

Matthew turned around to ask but God had already ascended back to Heaven. The lost boys approached the heavenly gates and strung the harp out front.

"Hey, who strung that harp?" The guardian angel called.

"We did," they boys replied.

"Well, state your business."

"We want to see God."

"God?" The angel gasped. "But nobody can see the great God. Nobody's ever seen the great God. I've never even seen him!"

"Didn't he just fucking float in here? If you've never seen him then how do you know there is one?" Luke asked defiantly.

"Number one, there is a backdoor and number two, you're wasting my time," the angel replied as he backed away from the gate.

"Oh please," begged Paul, "please sir, please, I've got to see the great and powerful God. Jonah of Galilee sent us!"

"Prove it!" The angel smirked.

"He's wearing the ruby red sneakers he gave us!" Mark shouted.

"Oh, well I'll be damned," said the angel in

disbelief. "Why didn't you say that in the first place? That's a horse of a different color. Come on in."

As the angel led the lost boys through the heavenly gates, they passed the Jerusalem bells-a-ringing, the roman Calvary choirs-a-singing and entered a dimly lit room. The space was just big for a large wooden table that would sit 12. On the table in front of each of them was a blue pill and a red pill. Suddenly the voice of God called out to them,

"Take ye of thee blue pill - and the story endeth, you shall wake up in your bed and believeth whatever you want to believeth. But taketh ye of thee red pill - and ye shall stay in Neverland and I will showeth thee how deepeth thee rabbit-hole goeth."

The boys looked at each other, nodded, and all simultaneously hollered "su woooo" and with that, God dispersed a red pill to each of them.

That day, the lost boys learned of the miraculous things Jesus had done throughout his life. God told them about how Jesus had fed 500 men and their families on just five barley loaves of bread and two fish. He told them about the Catalina Wine Mixer running out of wine during a wedding ceremony and how Jesus took all of the bottles of Fiji water and turned it to Moscato and Pinot. The boys learned about a possessed demon girl that Jesus healed and how Hollywood created a spinoff called The Exorcism of Emily Rose.

God explained how Jesus was conceived by the Holy Spirit, born of the Virgin Mary and fathered by Joseph through a weird twist of fate involving Mark Zuckerburg. God spared no detail because he wanted Jesus Christ's glory to be revealed so that the lost boys would truly believe in him.

To even further influence them of Jesus' awesomeness, God had the boys go down the river in a boat. (Which reminds me; Pete and Repeat were brothers. Pete and Repeat went down the river in a boat. Pete fell out, who was left? R _ _ _ _ t. Lambchop is the BOMB).

Once in the boat, the boys sat rolling, rolling on the river wondering what God had up his sleeve, (ha, God doesn't wear sleeves. Focus). Out of nowhere, a ghost-like image appeared just around the river bend. They couldn't believe their eyes; the ghost was literally walking on water and heading straight towards their boat.

The boys shrieked. "We gon' die," shouted Peter.

"Don't be afraid, it is I, Jesus," he said.

"Oh, well in that case, Lord, command me to

come upon the water and so that I may embrace thee," said Peter.

Jesus complied and made it so that Peter too could walk on water. It was just like TLC's Waterfalls music video except there weren't three black girls singing and dancing in puddles under a waterfall so really not just like that at all actually.

Peter took a few steps but got scared and began to sink, fast. Jesus reached out and saved him saying,

"Oh ye of little faith. Why did you doubt?"

The boys witnessing this from the boat began to worship and surrendered all, believing that this guy, Jesus Christ, *was* the real deal, son of God and, a bad motha- SHUT YO MOUTH - I'm just talking about Jesus. He was the holy messiah and they dubbed him King of the Jews.

From that point on, the lost boys became found

men and true followers of Christ.

They were now apostles and disciples. Their whole mission in life was to teach and spread the gospel of Christ.

- Forward track –

Following the gonorrhea, syphilis, herpes, massive diarrhea and six other plagues that befell The Pharaoh and his Detroit players, the Israelites began a traditional celebration known as Passover, (a Jewish festival celebrating Israelites freedom from slavery in Egypt).

It was that time of year again so Jesus sent his disciples into Neverland to meet a man carrying a jar of water. They all headed second star to the right and on till morning to a dive bar just outside of the old city. The men chose this particular pub because that was where Jesus was hosting his private holiday festivities.

What happened next is kind of a blur. More "he said, she said" than anything but, there are three sides to every story: my side, your side, and THE TRUTH. And the truth shall set you free. But, you can't handle the truth! So just keep reading.

Jesus sat down with his disciples for what was to be their last supper. In the corner of the room, a man named Leonardo da Vinci stood with a canvas capturing the moment through illustrative oil painting. He didn't usually do private parties but thought it might be worth something later. It was also a part of the VIP Passover Package that everyone in attendance got to take home a signed copy.

Jesus asked his disciples, "Do you remember in the movie *Indiana Jones: Temple of Doom* when Indy said, "YOU BETRAYED SHIVA" after that guy stole the Sankara stones? And then, the guy fell off the cliff and all the crocodiles ripped him to smithereens?"

They all nodded. Jesus went on to tell his disciples that one of them would soon betray him and that his betrayer would face a terrible death as well. Matthew then brought out the game "Guess Who" with all of their pictures on it.

"Let's get to the bottom of this," he said.

"No," Jesus replied. "Ain't nobody got time for that."

Jesus had really been looking forward to eating this Passover meal because they had flown in the cook from Roscoe's Chicken and Waffles and he was about to eat like he had never eaten before. He was also looking forward to it because he wanted his disciples to know that he was going to die a sacrificial death for their sins. He knew he would face impending doom as scriptures foretold:

"For God so loved the world that he gave his only begotten son, that whosoever believes in him should not perish, but have everlasting life. For God sent not his son into the world to condemn the world, but that the world through him might be saved."

He was going to establish a new covenant to replace the old one that the Jews had lived under for so long. His blood shed on Calvary would wash sins away. Basically, he wanted the celebration of Passover to remind people that he died so that they could live. Not in a cocky way though, just a "way it is" sort of way.

Jesus stood and said, "Do you this in remembrance of me."

He then broketh of the bread and handed a portion to each disciple.

"This is my body which is given for you. Eat ye all of it."

Jesus then grabbed a bottle of Ciroc.

"This is the token of God's new covenant to save you. It is sealed with blood and I will pour out to you. Shots, everybody."

They all clinked glasses. Some of the men began to cry. Paul sang to Jesus,

"Baby please don't goooo, if I wake up tomorrow will you still be here?"

Jesus sang back, "I don't want to leeeeave, but I gotta go right now. I'll be back before you know it."

Parting is such sweet sorrow.

Jesus and the Twelve Disciples were arrested following the last supper. The officers were so impressed by da Vinci's painting that they let him stay at the bar.

Jesus was held captive and mocked for being called the King of the Jews before being handed over for crucifixion. Crucifixions were generally regarded as shameful deaths reserved for people that challenged Roman's rule. Jesus did not cower in his trials because he knew that through his atonement for the sins of people in the world, salvation would be possible.

Jesus was tortured on a cross that hung between two convicted thieves who were also going to die that day.

"Father forgive them, for they know not what they do," Jesus uttered.

After Jesus' death, his body was removed and placed in a tomb. Before the sun set on the third day, Jesus rose from the dead. He came back like Jordan, wearing the four-five. He spent the next forty days telling people "I told you so" before he ascended into Heaven to sit at the right hand of his Father.

So, choose today whether you will live a life

serving God, die and go to Heaven OR if you will spend eternity in hades with the devil.

Start by repenting for laughing at this book SINNER.

Special Note: It is unclear what bunny rabbits, chocolate and candy have to do with Easter Sunday.

The end

ABOUT THE AUTHORS

Jocelyn Ingram is a 25 year old Californian who was born and raised in Lansing, Michigan. She is an avid people watcher who lives vicariously through Samantha Jones and Carrie Bradshaw. With a vivid imagination and extremely witty way with words, this is her first book.

Alayne Ingram is 32 years old and currently resides in Lansing, Michigan where she was born and raised. Cool story huh? She loves the game of basketball and although she has a job, apparently is also the family technology administrator and fun coordinator. Pro bono of course. This is her first book.